# RETURN FIRE

## CHRISTINA DIAZ GONZALEZ

SCHOLASTIC INC.

10 9 8 7 6 5 4 3 2 1          17 18 19 20 21

Printed in the U.S.A.   40
First printing 2017

Book design by Phil Falco

TO MAMI AND PAPI, MY CONSTANTS IN LIFE.
*LOS QUIERO* . . . TO THE MOON AND BACK.

# —ONE—

The sirens behind us wailed, growing louder with every passing second. I tightened my grip on the door handle. The police were closing in, and our old car wasn't built for a fast getaway.

"They're coming for us," I whispered to Asher. I inched down a little more in the backseat. "My dad said we couldn't trust anyone, including the police. We should make a run for it."

"Not yet." Asher scanned the streets, checking to see who was out there. "Those sirens might not have anything to do with us." He leaned forward, between the gap in the front seats, to talk to his old friend Gisak, who was driving us. "Think you can drive a little faster? We really need to get to the Knights of Malta compound quickly. Maybe go a different way?"

Gisak took a quick glance at the rearview mirror and then at the sea of red brake lights shining in front of us as traffic snarled to a standstill around the Roman Colosseum. "Why the big rush?"

Neither Asher nor I answered. There no way we could tell him the truth . . . He wouldn't believe it anyway. *I* could barely believe what had happened.

A few days ago, I'd been a normal American girl studying in Rome . . . but now my life was anything but normal. I had discovered that I was actually part of an ancient bloodline, one of the only people left in the world who could use the Spear of Destiny to change the future. Because of this, a secret organization called the Hastati wanted to kill me. Not only did this all sound crazy, but my life depended on making sure no one else found out about any of it.

"Are you in trouble or something?" Gisak prodded. "I might be able to help you. I'm quite resourceful you know, and I've been in my share of . . . *situations.*"

"The less you know the better," Asher answered. "But we can't just sit here in traffic. We need to go."

"Let's make a run for it," I whispered again. I was certain that the Hastati were right on our tail. We needed to be on the move. I knew getting to the Knights of Malta compound might take longer on foot, but at least we wouldn't be sitting ducks.

Asher shook his head. I didn't understand why he was being so stubborn.

"Asher, we've known each other a long time," Gisak said. "Don't you trust me?"

I stared at Asher. Gisak might be Asher's friend and he may have allowed Asher to use the secret tunnel that ran through his curio shop, but I'd learned the hard way that even friends could betray you.

My stomach clenched just thinking about how my own best friend, Simone, had betrayed me by stealing the spear away from us and giving it to her power-hungry mother. It was because of her that I now had to track down the spear again. If I didn't, the horrible vision I'd had of people dying would come true. Getting the spear was my only chance to change the future.

The sirens outside sounded like they were coming from every direction. We were running out of options, and Gisak wasn't helping. It was time to make a choice. I'd been told that choices determined destiny, and now I had to choose to take charge of my own fate.

I thrust open the door. "Let's go!" I said, darting out of the car.

BEEEEEP!

I froze as a police motorcycle came barreling toward me.

"Cassie!" Asher leaned out of the car and pushed me so hard that I went flying across to the far side of the sidewalk just as the motorcycle cop zoomed past me, blaring his horn.

"What do you think you're doing?" Asher yelled.

"But the cops, I thought they were . . ."

"Not everyone is after us . . . not yet anyway. There's probably an accident or something up ahead." He lowered his voice and spoke a little softer. "Look, I know you want to get the spear back, but we have to be careful. Think things through."

I nodded, realizing that I had to make better choices. I had already messed up once, when I used the spear: I thought that I was saving my father's life when in reality I had set up a chain of events that would cause thousands of people to die. It was the reason I had to get the spear back and fix everything. The fate of so many rested on it.

Gisak tapped the passenger seat's headrest as Asher and I both got back into the car. He studied me for a moment, then sighed. "All right. No more questions. You wanted fast; I'm going to give you fast."

Asher slammed the door as the car in front of us moved up a few feet.

"Hold on tight!" Gisak shouted as he gunned the engine and jumped the curb. Before we could say anything, Gisak maneuvered the car down the sidewalk, forcing a few pedestrians to jump out of the way, before turning onto a narrow, cobblestoned street. From there, he took several backstreets and alleyways until we arrived at the front of the massive door of the Priorato of the Knights of Malta.

Gisak parked next to a large tour bus. "One more chance to fill me in on what you're doing."

"Cassie has family here," Asher said, putting a hand on Gisak's shoulder. "We'll be fine. But thank you."

I watched as a few tourists wandered around the outside courtyard, waiting to take their turn peering through the door's keyhole. It was a well-known "secret" of Rome that visitors could see the dome of the Vatican perfectly lined up through the tunnel of trees on the other side of the compound's door.

They didn't suspect the truth.

That as they looked at the pretty view, something was looking at them. A retinal scanner that searched for people like me. A descendant of Saint Longinus, with the mark of the spear.

A person who could change destiny.

"Want me to wait for you here?" Gisak asked.

I opened the car door and shook my head. "No, we'll be fine once we're inside the compound."

At least I hoped we'd be. We were counting on Dame Elisabeth, the grandmother I had only met the day before, to help keep us safe while we came up with a plan for regaining the spear. She had saved my life once already, so it seemed like our best option.

"Asher"—Gisak grabbed Asher's backpack before he got out of the car—"you have to be careful." He glanced over at me. "Some people aren't always what they seem."

That was something he didn't need to tell us. We'd already experienced it. A stranger was my grandmother. My best friend was a traitor. I wasn't even who I thought I was.

Apparently, in my life, no one was who they appeared to be.

# —TWO—

Gisak was still watching us from his car when I looked through the keyhole of the Priorato. Just like the day before, I was greeted with the blinding flash of light reserved solely for those of us with the correct retinal pattern. Within a few minutes, I heard the clanking sound of someone opening the dead bolts on the door.

The tourists milling around us stopped to catch a glimpse of what was hidden behind the high walls that surrounded the compound.

The large door creaked open, revealing Dame Elisabeth, her gray hair pulled back by an elegant silk scarf. I could tell she was surprised to see us, but she didn't hesitate. She took a step forward and pulled me inside by the wrist. I turned to reach for Asher, making sure he wasn't left behind.

"I was so very worried about you, Cassandra," she whispered, drawing me close to her and squeezing my hand. Then she stepped away, gave the tourists a polite smile with a brief wave, and closed the door.

Standing inside the walls of the locked compound, I took a deep breath and slowly let it out. I hadn't realized how tense I was until that moment, when a wave of relief washed over me. A brief pit stop, enough to gather our thoughts and maybe get some information, was exactly what we needed.

"We're just glad you're here," Asher said, his shoulders relaxing a little.

Dame Elisabeth nodded, then looked back at me. "But why did you return? I mean, I'm glad you did, but"—she paused—"why come back here?"

I glanced over at Asher, unsure how much I should reveal. Should we tell her that we were here because the only other person who could help us was Asher's uncle, Brother Gregorio, but he had just died, leaving us on our own? What about telling her how we'd hoped Brother Gregorio would barter a peace with the Hastati once we had the spear? How much was too much?

"We first went to my uncle thinking he might be able to help us, but when we arrived at the monastery, he was . . . we found that . . . he had died," Asher said, his voice catching a little bit on the last word.

"We thought you might be able to help us instead," I said.

"Of course, of course." Dame Elisabeth nodded. "I'm sorry for your loss, but you said monastery. Your uncle is—?"

"Brother Gregorio of—"

Dame Elisabeth cut Asher off. "Gregorio is your uncle . . . Well, that certainly explains quite a bit." She sighed and looked out to the horizon. "So now it all begins again."

"Begins again?" I asked. "What do you mean?"

Her eyes narrowed as she evaluated the two of us. "Do you two know about Gregorio's connection to Tobias, the person who last controlled the spear?"

Asher nodded. "Yes, my uncle told me. He was Tobias's Guardian. His life was tied to Tobias's."

Just like Asher and me. I had bound him to my life when I used the spear. He was now my Guardian. If I used the spear and entered the Realm of Possibilities to change destiny, only Asher could bring me back to reality. And if I died, so did he.

Dame Elisabeth escorted us through one of the gardens. "So you also know that the Hastati were keeping Tobias in a coma to both prevent him from using the spear and keep the spear's power from going to someone else. They wouldn't allow him to wake up because of the things he had been doing with the power. He had become irrational. Obsessed with manipulating the future and wanting to bring about some kind of new world order."

A chill went down my spine. I didn't really know all the details about Tobias.

"My uncle explained all of that to me. He also knew that it wouldn't be long before Tobias died and that would mean his death, too. He was prepared." Asher spoke the words as though he'd memorized them but didn't truly believe them. I knew that no matter how much his uncle had warned him that this would happen, Asher hadn't been ready to lose the only family he had.

"Yes, but *we* are not prepared . . . not for how this will affect Cassandra." Dame Elisabeth rolled back her shoulders, her expression changing to what could only be described as soldier-like. "I had heard that Tobias was about to pass away.

Gregorio's death confirms it. Now the power of the spear can once again be claimed by any of the marked descendants."

I flinched but kept silent. It was best if no one—not even my grandmother—knew that I had already claimed the power of the spear.

"The Hastati will be even more desperate to find you," Dame Elisabeth continued. She stared at me, and then looked around the compound. "Everyone's gone through an extensive security check here, but I won't risk putting you in harm's way. Come with me." She strode away from the main building toward a small carport, the gravel under her feet crunching with each step.

"Wait, where are we going?" Asher asked, trotting alongside her. "I thought we'd be able to stay here. That you'd be able to protect Cassie."

"I'm not taking any chances." She gave me a sideways glance. "Not with my granddaughter."

"You're worried about the Knights?" I asked.

"Oh, no. The true Knights will protect you at all costs. It's everyone else that concerns me." We approached a black car parked in the carport, and Dame Elisabeth opened the car's back door. "With Tobias dead, you've become infinitely more valuable. You have a role to play, and that's why we're going somewhere only I know about. A safe house."

I stopped. "No. I'm not going to run away and hide." I needed to get the spear back and fix the future. Make sure that the final horrifying vision I'd seen didn't happen.

Staying out of sight might keep me safe, but it wasn't going to help undo the problems I'd created.

"My dear, this isn't running away. It's more of a regrouping . . . until we can sort some things out. Now let's get going."

Asher and I exchanged glances. We needed to tell her about Simone's mother taking the spear. That might alter whatever plan she was concocting. Perhaps she'd change her mind about running away.

"Dame Elisabeth, before we go, you need to know something," I said, trying to decide how much to tell her.

"You can talk to me when we're on our way."

"But it's about the spear," I explained. "We know where it is."

Dame Elisabeth's hand dropped from the car door. "What did you say?"

"The Spear of Destiny," Asher repeated. "Simone's mother, Sarah Bimington, has it. She may come after Cassie once she finds out that Tobias is dead and that Cassie is the only one who can use it."

"Sarah Bimington the financier?" Dame Elisabeth's eyes widened, and her gaze bounced back and forth between Asher and me. I could tell she didn't know whether to believe us or not. "What makes you think she's involved?"

"Because she stole it from us," I blurted.

"Actually," Asher corrected me, "Simone stole it, then gave it to her mother."

Dame Elisabeth raised her hand as if to slow down the conversation. "Hold on. The two of you had the spear? The actual spear?"

I nodded, not wanting to get into the details.

"But how did you get it? It's been missing for years."

All my muscles tightened. How was I supposed to answer this? I couldn't tell her we'd found the spear in her own garden and taken it without telling her. I hated having secrets from everyone—even the people I relied on. Asher was the only person I trusted.

As if reading my mind, Asher jumped in. "It involves my uncle," he lied. I gave him a grateful smile. "But that's not important right now. We just want you to tell the Hastati and the Knights so they can stop coming after Cassie and go after the spear."

"It's not that simple." Dame Elisabeth shook her head. "They'll need proof. *I* need proof."

"But the proof is that she has it!" I exclaimed.

"Cassandra, I believe that Simone took whatever spear you had in your possession, but that may not have been the real one. There are several replicas—"

"This wasn't a copy," Asher interrupted.

"How can you be sure?"

We couldn't tell her that the only way we knew for sure was that I had used the spear to change destiny. Grandmother or not, I didn't trust her with that fact.

"Brother Gregorio said so." Asher supplied the answer. "He would know the real one from a fake."

Dame Elisabeth paused to consider this. "That he would," she muttered. "Did you touch the spear, Cassandra? Even for a moment?"

"No," I said, adding to the lies. "Asher was the one who held it."

"But you felt its pull, didn't you? Like a magnet drawing you closer."

I nodded. That, at least, was true. I hadn't known how to explain the sensation, but that was a pretty close description. It was like a chocolate craving, but way more intense. I could still feel it now. I itched to get into action and get the spear back from Sarah Bimington so I could use it again.

"That's what I thought." Her lips tightened. "All right, I'll make a call as soon as we get to where we're going."

I didn't have a better plan, so I gave Asher a little nod and we climbed into the backseat of the car. I'd told my father to meet us at the compound, but I could call him, too, once we got to our destination, and update him on our whereabouts.

Dame Elisabeth slid into the driver's seat and turned the key, but she kept the car in park as she pressed a button on the sun visor. The entire car began to shake. "Hold on."

"Wait! What's happening? What is this?" I gripped the sides of the seat as the car descended like an elevator, dropping several floors. Once we hit the bottom, a whirring sound filled the cavernous space around us. I looked out the window just as a metal panel closed up the hole we had dropped into, leaving us in total darkness.

Dame Elisabeth turned on the headlights, revealing a tunnel in front of us. "This, my dear, is our way out." She revved the engine. "I'm making sure no one can follow us."

*This cannot be real*, I thought.

Speeding through an underground secret tunnel felt like we were in a spy movie. Except there was no guarantee that the good guys would win. I didn't even know if we would survive.

All of a sudden, a pain shot through the right side of my skull, making me wince. It felt like my head was about to explode. I wanted to move or call for help, but I couldn't. I was paralyzed.

My heart raced and I couldn't seem to catch my breath. I saw flashes of different images. At first they seemed random, but then I realized they were all from the vision I'd had when I used this spear. Like a slideshow quickly flipping through pictures, I could barely make out one image before it changed to another. For a split second, I saw myself in a boat sailing by a beautiful town with white and cream-colored buildings that ran down the side of the mountain all the way to the shoreline. Then the image of a man standing by a wide, rounded window appeared. Before I could gather my thoughts, a sharp jolt of electricity ran through my elbow. Just like that, the images vanished.

The pain in my head had also disappeared, and now all I was left with was a tingling sensation in my hand.

I looked down at my arm and realized that a sharp turn by Dame Elisabeth had caused me to hit my funny bone against the door, snapping me out of whatever trance I'd been in.

"Everything okay?" Asher looked at me.

"Yeah. I think so," I muttered, stretching out my arm to get feeling back in my fingertips. I wasn't sure what had just happened, but it was gone now. The only thing that remained was the knowledge that something having to do with the spear was still happening to me.

And my gut told me it was something bad.

I wanted to tell Asher everything I'd seen. Maybe he could help me make sense of it. But I was afraid to say too much while we were with Dame Elisabeth. I sunk back into the leather seat, waiting for my heart to slow to normal.

A few minutes later, she pulled the car into a side passage and brought it to a stop. A panel above us slid open, letting in a faint light, and the floor rose on some type of lift. When it all stopped, we found ourselves in the middle of a messy and cramped garage.

"Is this it?" Asher put his hand on the door handle. "The safe house?"

"Not quite. Stay put." Dame Elisabeth got out and went to a wall lined with shelves that held paint cans, tools, and other junk.

She tilted a can forward, and the wall slid back to reveal a hidden room. Flicking on a light, she grabbed a large duffel bag and stuffed it with a laptop, some other electronic equipment, and a small leather backpack.

My mouth popped open in surprise. This very proper-looking woman was so much more than what she appeared. My grandmother was hard-core.

Tossing everything in the trunk of the car, she returned to the driver's seat. "Now we're ready to go to the safe house," she said.

We exited the garage and made a right turn onto one of Rome's busy streets. Dame Elisabeth spoke up again. "I should've asked you before, but neither of you have a cell phone or any other electronics on you, right?"

"I have one, but it can't be traced and I haven't used it," Asher said.

Dame Elisabeth lowered the window next to him. "Toss it."

"But it's a burner phone. We might need—"

She slammed on the brake, sending me crashing into the back of her seat.

A car honked and swerved in order to avoid ramming us from behind, but Dame Elisabeth ignored it.

"Toss it," she repeated, looking back at him with a deadly serious expression. "My orders aren't up for discussion. Understand?"

I nudged Asher. We needed her help, which meant doing what she asked of us.

Asher grimaced as he threw the phone toward the sidewalk.

"Good." Dame Elisabeth started the car again and focused on the road ahead. "I can't take the chance of having any electronics traced when we get on the highway toward Malafede. We'll be there soon."

"Malafede?" Having been in Rome for less than a year, I was still unfamiliar with the names of the different neighborhoods and suburbs that surrounded the city. "Do you have an apartment there?"

"It's not in the city," Asher said, his face tense with worry. "Malafede is a national park. There's nothing out there."

"Don't worry, I have a small cottage hidden away near the lowlands. I used to go there for bird-watching and to escape the city." Dame Elisabeth smiled. "No one will find us. It's very secluded."

Asher shook his head in silent disapproval. "But if they do," he muttered, "no one will hear us scream, either."

# —THREE—

At first Malafede was a place of large open fields and only small patches of shrubs and trees. Then, gradually, the forest became more dense. There was a sense of solitude and peace in the air, and I could see why Dame Elisabeth chose to come here.

When we pulled up to the cottage itself, it was almost exactly what I'd expected of a small place tucked among the trees in the middle of nowhere: tiny rooms, wooden floors, and not much furniture. We had taken several dirt roads in order to get there, and I could see why Dame Elisabeth considered the place a secure location. But Asher was right: The isolation made us vulnerable.

Once inside, Dame Elisabeth flipped a large lever on the wall next to the front door. "All right. The security system is now armed and ready."

"A house alarm?" I asked.

"No, better than that. A perimeter alarm that circles the property with an invisible fence about a kilometer out. It'll give us a few minutes' warning if someone approaches the area." She yanked off a large white cloth that was draped over a leather couch, kicking a cloud of dust into the air.

"Where do I put this?" Asher had lugged the large duffel bag into the house. I could tell he was straining a bit to hold it up.

"You can set it down over there." Dame Elisabeth pointed to a small table next to the kitchen. "Thank you."

"Won't animals trigger the alarm?" I asked. "I'm sure there are some wandering around here."

Dame Elisabeth unzipped the bag and pulled out a bunch of electronic equipment, including the laptop, and placed it on the kitchen table. "No, it emits a high-frequency sound that scares off most animals. Humans can't hear it." She glanced up at Asher, who was hovering over the table of electronics. She snapped a wire into place and gave him a stern glare. "Make sure you don't touch any of this. It's very sensitive."

Asher raised his hands and took a step back.

"This place is nice," I observed, trying to keep the peace. I sat down in a wooden rocking chair by the window. It was beautifully carved, and placed with a view of the fireplace and of the woods out the window. The whole space was rugged, yet refined. Like my grandmother.

"Yes, well, the cabin isn't really designed for more than two people, but we'll make do." She adjusted some dials on one of the boxes, then focused on Asher and me. "There's a bedroom over there with a bed big enough for Cassie and me to share, and, Asher, you can sleep on the sofa tonight until we make other arrangements for you."

"I'm not leaving Cassie," he said matter-of-factly.

"Well, you're a minor, and your family—"

"I have no family. Not anymore." I could hear the sadness in his voice. "And I'm not leaving Cassie."

Dame Elisabeth eyed the two of us for a moment. "Very well," she replied, turning her attention to the laptop. "In the meantime, you can make yourself useful and get some wood for the fireplace. The cottage can get a bit chilly at night."

"Um . . ." Asher stayed where he was. He silently mouthed to me, "Should I go?"

I couldn't see the harm in him going, and I certainly wasn't afraid to stay with Dame Elisabeth by myself. I nodded my approval.

"There's a shed about fifty yards toward the back. You should be able to find an ax and some logs to chop back there."

"Yes, ma'am," Asher replied, and headed outside.

"And, Cassie," Dame Elisabeth added without looking up from the electronic gadgets, "you can check out the kitchen and take stock of what food we have."

There wasn't much to take stock of because most of the food was survival-style, military-looking food packages that didn't expire for another fifteen years. All the packages were covered with a heavy layer of dust. It was obvious she hadn't been here in a while.

"You have twenty-seven meal packages," I reported a few minutes later. "Four of them say chicken and rice, but the rest are beef Stroganoff." I couldn't help making a face, but immediately regretted doing so. I knew it made me seem very immature. I pointed to the equipment on the table. "What is this stuff exactly?"

"Our link with the outside world. Not even the Hastati can access it." She smiled. "The finest satellite technology that China, Russia, and the US military can supply."

"Wow."

Dame Elisabeth swiveled to face me. "I'm sending an encrypted message to a friend. He's going to make sure that your information about Sarah Bimington reaches the Hastati and the Knights."

I still wasn't completely over the shock of learning that I had a grandmother, let alone the fact that she was involved with the Knights of Malta, but this took things to another level.

"Don't look so surprised, Cassandra. You come from a line of very strong, resourceful women." She smiled warmly at me, her eyes crinkling at the sides. "We know how to answer the call when the time is right. You will, too."

"What call?" Asher asked, coming into the room, arms heaped high with logs and kindling.

Dame Elisabeth shifted her gaze to him, but the soft look stayed on her face. "Whatever we're called to do in this life. The Lord has plans for each of us . . . It's all a matter of choosing which path to follow."

Choices. That was my problem. I had only used the spear once, and that one choice had apparently set the world on a path toward destruction. Again I thought of the visions I'd seen when I'd entered the Realm of Possibilities. Of the one that still haunted me: people in hazmat suits walking among scores of dead bodies that littered the streets of Rome . . .

I couldn't let it happen. I had to get the spear back and reenter the Realm of Possibilities so I could choose a different future.

"Cassie. Cassie." Dame Elisabeth touched my arm. "Are you okay?"

"Huh?" I snapped back to the moment at hand. My skin was covered in goose bumps.

"You seemed lost in your thoughts," she said.

I fiddled with the ring Brother Gregorio had made me wear, and then stopped, remembering it was embedded with a poison that could kill me. "I was just thinking about everything that's happened. Nothing else."

"Mm-hm." Dame Elisabeth studied me for a few seconds. "Well, I see the Hastati already have you both wearing their rings. I'll see if I can find a way to remove them without releasing the venom."

I couldn't believe she knew what the rings were.

"How do you know about these things?" Asher asked, staring down at his own finger.

She smirked. "There's not much about the Hastati that I don't know."

"Here, have a seat," she said, pulling out the chair next to her. "Instead of talking about the rings, why don't you tell me about what happened to you? We have some time."

"I'm not sure where to start," I said, sitting down next to her.

"Let's begin with Simone. Tell me about how she stole the spear."

"Um, okay." I glanced across the room at Asher. He was sprawled on the sofa, watching us intently. "It was . . . well, she used to be . . ." I tried to gather my thoughts, still unsure if I understood everything that had happened. "Simone helped her mother take it from us—but I don't think she was really planning on stealing it . . . at least not in the beginning."

"We don't know that for sure," Asher interjected. "I think it was part of her plan, or her mother's plan, all along. Get us to trust her, and then, when we let our guard down, that's when she'd betray us."

"No." I faced him. "You don't know her like I do. She was my best friend. When we found Brother Gregorio dead, she probably panicked."

"So, she secretly called her mother while we weren't looking, filled her in on everything having to do with the Hastati, and then handed over the spear to her . . . all because she panicked? Without consulting either one of us." He shook his head. "C'mon, Cassie, just admit it. Simone's not the person you thought she was. She was never really your friend."

I jumped up. "How would you know? You met us both a couple of days ago. You have no idea who either of us are!"

Asher's jaw muscles tensed. "I know you, Cassie. I knew you before we ever met."

"What does that mean?" I said, exasperated with him. "You don't even make sense."

"He means that he's your Guardian, Cassie." Dame Elisabeth smiled, unbothered by our argument.

"Huh? Yeah, well . . . but . . ." I stammered, thinking that she might have also figured out that I was bound to the spear. I glanced at Asher.

"I can see by your reaction that this is something you both already knew. I'm guessing Gregorio informed you of it."

Once again, Asher intervened. "Yes, my uncle told me it was what I was born to do. That everyone who is marked and becomes bound to the spear has a Guardian. And that being a Guardian to Cassie would be my role to fill one day . . . if she ever became bound." His eyes were focused right on me, even while he spoke to Elisabeth. "That's why I knew about her even before we met. Before she knew what her role would be."

"I was never told anything about who I was," I muttered. My dad had spent years trying to locate the spear, but had never told me the truth about my heritage. My thoughts turned back to my dad, who we'd left lying in a hospital room. I'd told him to meet us at the Knights of Malta compound, and I'd meant to get in touch with him sooner. By now he could already have gotten there, only to find me gone!

"Wait!" I exclaimed, turning to Dame Elisabeth. "I need to get in touch with my father, before we do anything else."

"Your father?" A concerned look flashed across Dame Elisabeth's face.

"Yes." I turned to Asher. "We need to let him know that I'm okay. That our plans changed."

Asher nodded. "We could have someone go to him or leave a message at the Priorato."

"One minute. Are you talking about . . . ?" Dame Elisabeth left the end of the question up in the air as if she was afraid to finish it.

"My father. His name's Felipe Arroyo, and we left him at a hospital."

"Oh, I see." Dame Elisabeth's shoulders relaxed and dropped a bit. "He is ill, I take it?"

"No, not really," I explained, not understanding why Dame Elisabeth looked so relieved. "I mean, he was recovering from a gunshot wound and all, but what stopped him from coming with us was some drug he was given. He was still too weak to walk when one of the Hastati's assassins showed up. We had to leave, but I told him to meet us at the Priorato. He'll freak out if I'm not there."

"I'll make sure word gets to him that you're safe." Dame Elisabeth faced the equipment on the table. "We don't want him stirring things up."

"Wait a minute." Asher eyed her carefully. "Who did you think Cassie was talking about?"

"Her father, as she said," Dame Elisabeth answered. "I simply didn't know his name."

But it seemed clear that wasn't it. She'd gotten ruffled when I mentioned contacting my father. I had seen the confusion on her face when I talked about Papi. Suddenly, it dawned on me.

"My biological father," I said. "That's who you thought I was talking about."

Dame Elisabeth stayed quiet and continued typing.

"You know who he is . . . don't you?" Asher took a few steps to stand next to me.

Her posture stiffened and she shifted in her seat.

I put my hand on her shoulder. "Please, I need to know who he is. There've been too many secrets already."

She stayed still for another moment, then turned and took my hand in hers. "Yes, yes, you do. But you have to understand that you are nothing like him. You are your mother's daughter . . . I can see it in your eyes . . . you aren't his."

Excitement welled up inside me. Obviously, Dame Elisabeth didn't like him, but maybe this person would help us get the spear back. His blood ran through my veins, and it was that connection that had led me to accidentally save him from the brink of death when I thought I was saving Papi. My biological father might even know how to use the spear's power to change what I'd seen in my visions. This could be the break we'd been waiting for!

Dame Elisabeth sighed. "Your father is—was—Tobias."

My heart fell. I could feel the room swirling, and I stumbled back.

It couldn't be. Tobias was a madman who wanted to destroy the world. He was evil. He had tried to use the power of the spear to bring on the apocalypse.

No, I told myself, this couldn't be true.

I took a deep, shaky breath and looked to Dame Elisabeth

to tell me she had made a mistake. But she was watching me with pity in her eyes.

I was the daughter of a monster.

And, what was worse, I had brought that monster back from the dead.

# —FOUR—

Asher had a look of horror on his face as his eyes met mine. He knew what this meant.

Tobias wasn't dead after all.

The spear had misled me. I had thought I was using it to save my father, Felipe Arroyo, but it seemed like he'd never been in danger of dying. It had been Tobias's death that I had sensed . . . and his life that I saved.

The power of the spear must have come to me the moment he died, and then I brought him back to life by mistake.

"Are you sure?" I squeaked out the words. "He's my father?"

"Yes." Dame Elisabeth motioned for me to sit down. "How much do you know about Tobias?"

I swallowed the lump in my throat. "I know that he killed people and had some crazy plan to get rid of most of the people on the planet." I shook my head. "I can't be related to him."

"Well, Tobias wasn't always like that. Your mother loved him. He was charismatic and handsome. A real charmer." She sighed. "And I do believe he loved her. But he changed after becoming bound to the spear." She glanced away, recalling something from the past. "There was something ugly inside him. He slipped down a dark path . . . one where even she couldn't reach him. In the end, she only feared him."

I had so many questions. About my mother, about my background, and now about Tobias. How had the spear changed him? Would it change me, too? These were things only Dame Elisabeth would know. "Is that why my mother left Italy?" I asked. "Why she ended up in the US with my dad . . . the one who raised me? Did she have it all planned out?"

"Yes, to some extent." Dame Elisabeth stared at me for a moment and then shook her head slightly. "I'm sorry. It's just that you remind me so much of her. It's like going back in time." She reached over and gently stroked my cheek. "I want to get to know you, Cassandra. I truly do. You're meant for great things, and I want to help you achieve them."

I was still trying to process everything when the laptop made a pinging noise, and a message popped up on the screen. Dame Elisabeth turned her attention to it. I tried to sneak a look, but the words made no sense. It was all in code.

She entered a response, but the letters changed to asterisks as she typed, hiding them from my view.

"Was that about my dad?" I asked as she finished her message. "Felipe Arroyo," I clarified, not wanting there to be any confusion with Tobias.

"No." Dame Elisabeth walked across the room and pulled out a gun from the small leather backpack that had been in the duffel bag. "I'm working on getting us more food and supplies." She took the weapon to the bedroom where I could hear her opening a drawer.

Asher and I exchanged looks. We needed to talk and figure out what our next step was going to be, but that couldn't happen with Dame Elisabeth nearby. We'd have to wait for the right moment.

Dame Elisabeth walked back into the room with a bulky square phone in her hand.

"Thought we couldn't have phones here," Asher said. "Isn't that why you made me throw mine away?"

"This is a specialized satellite phone. It's different." She walked toward the front door. "I just need to make this call, and then we can continue our talk, Cassandra."

She stepped outside and pointed the phone's antenna up to the sky.

Asher closed the door and turned to face me.

"I had no idea about Tobias," I blurted. "I would never have—"

"I know, I know."

"He's alive because of me. Those horrible things I saw for the future, they might have something to do with him. I let him back out into the world again."

"You had no idea you were saving him. It was a mistake, Cassie. We'll figure out a way to fix it once we get the spear." The determination in Asher's voice gave me hope. He was walking around the table, carefully inspecting each piece of electronic equipment as he spoke. "But this also changes things with Simone's mom. I thought she'd come after you once she found out Tobias was dead, but now that he's still alive . . ."

"You think it might buy us some more time?" I thought it through. "Yeah, if she thinks he's still bound to the spear, she'll be trying to get to him. He's exactly the kind of person who would work with her to use the spear for their own power or wealth or—" I broke off. Simone's mom already had more power and wealth than most of the people in the world. How could she want more? I rested my hand on one of the boxes and accidentally flipped off one of the switches.

"Careful!" Asher reached across and turned the box back on.

I stepped away and went to the window. Dame Elisabeth was pacing around the car, still talking on the phone. "Do you think the Hastati know that Tobias lost the power?" I asked him.

"I don't know. In your vision, were there other people in the room when he died?"

I thought back to the scene I'd witnessed. Nurses and doctors clustered around Tobias. It was why I hadn't been able to see who was in the hospital bed; I had simply felt that it was my father. "Yeah, there were."

"Then the Hastati probably know that he lost the power." Asher pursed his lips together. "Which means you're in as much danger from them as ever."

"But won't they be focused on getting the spear? Dame Elisabeth told them who has it."

"Yeah, sure. But they can't take the chance that Simone's mom might get both the spear and someone who can control it. They'll have to hurry up and eliminate everyone with the birthmark . . . including you and Tobias." He closed the drapes. "I don't think we should stay here. As soon as Dame

Elisabeth comes back in, we need to convince her that the best thing to do is go after the spear. The Hastati may have even killed Tobias by now."

"No . . . I don't think so." I recalled one of the images of the future that had flashed in front of me while I held the spear. "Not yet anyway."

Asher sat down on the sofa. "What do you mean?"

"When I used the spear . . ." I sat next to him and closed my eyes, trying to bring it all back. "The images came and went very fast."

"Uh-huh."

"I had asked to know when I'd see my father again. But I saw a stranger. I saw a man standing by a window, looking out at the sea, and I was walking toward him. It didn't make sense at the time because I was expecting to see my dad. But that stranger must have been—"

"Tobias."

I nodded. "Yeah. I guess it showed me my biological father . . . but he was definitely alive. I'd need to see a photograph or something of him to be sure, but if what the spear showed me really will happen, then I'll meet him one day."

Asher sighed. "Yeah, so we'll definitely need Dame Elisabeth to give us some info on him."

"I think I can get her to fill us in since—"

The door swung open, and Dame Elisabeth stormed into the cottage. Her eyes were blazing with anger.

"You!" She pointed to me. "You think you can play me for the fool?"

My mouth went dry, and I suddenly felt very vulnerable. "What?" Clearly, someone on the phone had said something about me. But what exactly had caused her to get so angry?

"Pretending to be so naïve . . . you almost had me believing that you knew nothing of what was happening."

"I . . . uh . . . why would I . . . I mean, I have no idea . . ."

"Stop." She held up her hand. "Enough of the acting."

"Dame Elisabeth." Asher took a step forward. "If you'll just tell us what you are talking about, then maybe we can understand what has you so upset."

She rolled back her shoulders, smoothed her hair, and regained her composure. The flash of anger was gone, replaced by an icy stare that sent a shiver down my spine. I was reminded that though she might be my grandmother, I barely knew this woman.

"Let me try this again," she said, her eyes fixed on me. "I've just been informed that Tobias is alive . . . and that he's escaped from where the Hastati were holding him."

"Escaped?" I couldn't believe it.

"How?" Asher asked with equal surprise. "Weren't the Hastati guarding him?"

Dame Elisabeth's eyes narrowed. "Someone from the outside broke him out of the facility."

"Simone's mother," I muttered.

"Most likely," Dame Elisabeth agreed. "But isn't it interesting how neither one of you seems shocked that Tobias is actually alive, only that he escaped. It's as if you both knew that he hadn't died with Gregorio. Would either of you care to elaborate on how you already knew this?"

We stayed silent.

"Well, why don't I tell you my theory?" She looked at us, lips pressed firmly together, giving us one last chance to speak. But we didn't. "According to my sources, Tobias did die . . . albeit momentarily, but then, somehow, he spontaneously made a full recovery. They say it was as if something . . . or someone had miraculously restarted his heart."

"But maybe he didn't actually die," Asher suggested. "Perhaps your source was wrong."

"Doubtful." Dame Elisabeth took a seat and slid the laptop to the opposite side of the kitchen table. "I believe his heart did stop and then someone changed his fate."

I couldn't help looking at Asher. Were we busted? Should we confess? Our plan had been to deny everything and not tell anyone that I was bound to the spear. The only problem was, if Dame Elisabeth had figured it out so quickly, then others within the Hastati would know, too. Denial no longer seemed to be a good strategy.

Dame Elisabeth leaned back in the chair, her eyes narrowing into tiny slits as she stared at me. "Cassandra, I know you must have used the spear to save Tobias. The question now becomes . . . what else are you willing to do?"

# —FIVE—

Silence filled the room. I could only hear my heart beating as Dame Elisabeth stared at me, waiting for a reply that I didn't want to give.

"Well?" Dame Elisabeth raised a single eyebrow. "Don't you have anything to say?"

I stayed quiet.

"Cassandra, possessing the power of the spear is a life-long commitment and you will need training. I can help . . . but don't insult me with any more denials or lies."

It seemed like we were busted and, truth be told, I couldn't think of a better ally. She was an assassin-fighting, techno-savvy, Hastati-knowing grandmother who wanted to help.

With no options left, I decided to come clean. Dame Elisabeth stayed quiet as I told her everything from finding the spear in the Knights of Malta garden to misusing it while trying to save my adopted father. I only left out the part about putting the world in danger. I told her I didn't see anything after the events I changed. It was bad enough for her to know that I had resurrected World Enemy Number One—she didn't need to know that the granddaughter she had just met was an even bigger screwup.

Finally, when I'd finished, she stood and walked to the window. The setting sun cast an orange light on her face. "To think this all started because your mother chose to hide the spear instead of giving it to me." She shook her head. "She was so stubborn."

I got a weird feeling in the pit of my stomach. I hadn't stopped to consider my mother's thinking in all of this. *Why hadn't she trusted Dame Elisabeth with her secret? Why had she hidden the spear, and why hadn't she told Dame Elisabeth its location? Had I been too quick to tell so much?*

Dame Elisabeth was lighting a gas lantern that hung on a hook by the door, when she glanced over at me. "Don't look so worried, Cassandra. Just remember that the spear only allows you to control the immediate future, but in time, you'll see how changing small events can lead to larger ramifications. We'll work together on this. I can help you . . . You won't be like Tobias." She headed toward the kitchen with the light. "Now, why don't the two of you start a fire while I make us some dinner? It's dark enough outside that the smoke won't be seen."

I hesitated. I didn't want the conversation with her to end. Did she really think I'd be able to learn to use the spear to make changes? What if part of my destiny was to be like Tobias? I shared his genes after all. Or had the fact that Papi raised me changed things?

I wanted . . . no, *needed* to know more about both my biological parents. It was the only way to know more about myself.

Asher seemed to sense what I was thinking. "She's right about you not being like him. You used the spear to *save* someone . . . don't forget that."

"Yeah, but I knew there would be consequences and I didn't care," I whispered.

"Well, maybe you're like your mom," Asher suggested. "Or better yet, maybe you're like yourself and it has nothing to do with where you come from."

"But that's part of the problem . . . I don't know where I come from. The only family I grew up hearing about was my dad's family in Cuba . . . and now I know that they aren't even related to me."

"Then go talk to her," he said, motioning to the kitchen, where Dame Elisabeth had started cooking. "Find out. I'll stay here and get the fire going."

I walked to the tiny kitchen. There was barely room for one person to move around, so I hovered by the doorway. My grandmother had a pot of boiling water on the one-burner stove while she opened a package of beef Stroganoff. "Dame Elisabeth, can I ask you some questions about my mother?"

"Perhaps you should call me something else," she said, lowering the flame on the gas stove. "Dame Elisabeth sounds a bit too formal."

"Um . . . Grandmother?" I asked.

"Ugh, no. We'll think of another name." She poured the contents of the package into the pot and stirred. "So, you mentioned some questions . . . What is it you want to know?"

"Our family . . ." I said simply. "Who are they?"

"What do you mean?"

"It's just that I grew up thinking my background was Cuban, but I guess that's not true. So, what am I really? Do I have other relatives? What about my grandfather?"

Dame Elisabeth wiped her hands on a dishrag next to the small kitchen sink. "Our family is . . . I guess you would call us a bit nomadic. My parents, your great-grandparents, were Armenian and Spanish, but I was born in France, grew up in Spain, and moved to Cuba when I was in my twenties. There's really no other family to speak of, since my parents and your grandfather died long ago." She cut open another package of prepared food. "I raised your mother by myself in Cuba until she was . . ." She glanced over at me. "Well, until she was about your age, so I suppose your feeling Cuban is still pretty accurate. She considered herself more Cuban than anything else."

"Well, I see myself as American . . . but I know what you mean. Why did you leave Cuba? Did you know my dad . . . Felipe?"

"Yes, I knew Felipe in Cuba. He was a friend of your mother's." She poured another beef Stroganoff dinner into the pot. "As for why I left . . . it was because of work. I started working with the Knights and a few other organizations that required I move to Italy."

I leaned against the wall. "What exactly do you do for them?"

She smiled. "I'm what you might call a consultant."

"Consulting on what?"

"Sensitive things that require a certain finesse." She ripped a few paper towels and folded them into napkins. She handed them to me along with three forks. "But that's not really important. What is important is that you eat something tonight so we can get started on your training tomorrow."

I eyed the food now bubbling along with the water inside the pot. It didn't look appetizing, but I was hungry enough not to care. "What kind of training?" I asked, envisioning her teaching me some self-defense moves.

"Mental conditioning. Here." She grabbed a notepad. "Why don't we start right now?" Pulling out a pen from one of the drawers, she drew what looked like a river with a small boat. "Now pay attention, Cassandra. You have to figure this out for yourself. No help from Asher. Ready?"

I nodded.

Dame Elisabeth pointed to one side of the page. "On this side of the river, you have a farmer, a wolf, a chicken, and a bag of chicken seed." Dame Elisabeth sketched all four on the left side. "And on the opposite side of the river, there's the farmer's new house. The farmer needs to take the wolf, the chicken, and the seed to his place, but he can only take one item at a time across the river." She glanced up at me to make sure I was following along. "What is the least amount of trips it will take the farmer to have everything at his new place?"

I wasn't sure why she was asking this, but I quickly answered, "Three."

"Really? What does he take across first?"

"He takes the seed and then—"

"No," she interrupted. "The wolf would eat the chicken if they're left alone. Try again."

"Oh." I studied the drawing a little more, catching on to the tricky part of the question. "The farmer would have to take the chicken first, because if he takes the wolf first, then the chicken would eat the bag of seeds."

"Mm-hm." She smiled. "Go on."

"Then he'd have to bring over . . ." I scrunched my eyebrows, realizing there was an even bigger problem to the puzzle. "Wait, no matter what's brought over, whether it's the seed or the wolf, when the farmer goes back for the third item, something will get eaten. Either the chicken or the seed."

"Seems like a bit of a quandary." She turned her back to me and continued making dinner. "Give it some more thought."

I stared at the drawing for a while, but I couldn't find a solution.

"Does it have an answer?" I asked, frustrated that I couldn't figure it out.

"It certainly does. You just need to think about each future consequence and all the options. This is part of getting you ready."

"Ready for what?"

"For what you were born to do . . . Using the spear to ensure that the world follows the right path."

There was nothing I could say in response. I had used the spear once and already messed things up in a major way. I only wanted to use the spear to fix what I'd done—and that was it. I wasn't the person she thought I was.

After dinner, and a few more brain games, Dame Elisabeth checked the coded messages on her laptop. "I need to make another call," she announced, picking up the satellite phone. "I'll be right back."

The moment the door shut behind her, Asher turned to me. "Cassie, I don't think it's safe to stay here. We can call the number my uncle had written in his red address book. The one he told me to call in case he died."

"But we don't know who that might be or what they would do." I pulled back the curtain and glanced outside. It was pitch dark, and I couldn't see much of anything. "At least for tonight, I think this is the best place. We can figure out what to do tomorrow."

Suddenly, a dark silhouette crossed in front of the window causing me to jump back.

The door opened, and Dame Elisabeth motioned for me to come closer. She had a scowl on her face, and her hand covered the bottom of the phone.

"Cassandra, your father is on the phone. He—"

"Papi? You got ahold of him? Is he okay? Let me talk to him." I reached for the phone, but Dame Elisabeth pulled back.

"He's fine, but he's being a bit unreasonable about you being here. You have to calm him down." She stared at me, making sure I understood. "Don't give away anything about where we are . . . Someone could be listening," she said, passing me the satellite phone. "Make him understand that it's better this way."

I took the phone, anxious to hear my dad's voice. "Papi?" There was no answer, only static. "Papi?" I asked again.

"Outside." Dame Elisabeth held the door open for me. "And point the antenna straight up." She followed me out.

Once we were about twenty feet away from the house, the

crackling on the phone subsided, and I heard my father's voice. "Hello? Hello? Is anyone still there?" he asked.

"Papi, it's me," I answered.

"*¡M'ija!* Are you okay? They won't tell me where you are. I thought we were going to meet . . . where you said."

He knew our conversation might be monitored and was being careful. Dame Elisabeth didn't have to worry. My father understood all too well what was at stake.

"I'm safe. Don't worry." I glanced at Dame Elisabeth, who gave me an approving nod, before returning her gaze to the forest around us. "How are you?"

"I'm fine, but that's not what's important." His voice was laden with concern, and I imagined him running his fingers through his graying dark hair, like he did whenever he was worried. "I was about to leave the clinic and meet you, but . . ."

I heard a muffled voice in the background, and my father responded, "I know, I know."

"Papi, who's there with you?" The thought that the half-eared man might have returned for my father filled me with dread. "Is someone forcing you to say things?"

"Huh? Oh . . . no, no. We just have to be careful with what we say."

"But the person who's there with you, does he have both ears? I know that sounds crazy, but just say yes or no."

"Yes, don't worry." He paused for a moment, and I could hear more muffled conversation. "I'll be leaving here with him, but I want him to bring me to you. We can go back to the US."

The offer was so tempting. We could go back to the life

I'd known, just the two of us . . . but I knew that what had started here would follow me wherever I went. "No, Papi, I can't." It was up to me to change the path I'd accidentally created, to stop all the destruction I'd seen in my vision.

"But over there it'll be easier to hide . . . until this is over."

"Papi," I sighed, "it'll never be over. Someone will always be after me. Because of who I am."

"No, that's not true. I can keep you safe. Let me speak to that woman."

"Papi, I have a job to do here. I'm not leaving . . . not yet."

"You're too young to be making those decisions, Cassie. Let me talk to her . . . now."

"But—"

"No buts. Put her on now. *Ahora*."

I handed the phone back to my grandmother.

"Satisfied?" she asked him.

I could hear my father's voice rising on the other end. He was not giving up.

"Mr. Arroyo." Dame Elisabeth's voice had a sharp tone to it. "You may think you remember me from when you were a child in Cuba, but trust me, you have no idea what I am capable of."

My father was not backing down, and I could hear him arguing with her.

"No," Dame Elisabeth stopped him. "You thought your job was to protect Cassie, but you were wrong. It's our job to make her strong enough to protect herself." She paused for a second, her eyes locking with mine. "And then she can protect the world."

# —SIX—

Nothing could be said to convince my father that I should be left alone under the protection of a woman he barely knew. Finally, Dame Elisabeth agreed to bring him to the cottage the next morning, along with some supplies.

I was glad he was going to be with me, but I knew he'd try to keep me from going after the spear. Which meant that even though I loved him more than anything, I'd have to go against his wishes. I had to fix my mistakes, and that meant using the spear again.

All night, I lay awake next to Dame Elisabeth thinking of what to do next. Just like in that stupid riddle with the farmer taking things across the river, every idea had bad consequences. Eventually, my eyelids grew heavy, but although I was physically drained, I couldn't rest. Every time I drifted off, nightmare details from my vision jarred me awake. Then, just before dawn, I slipped into darkness.

I woke with a pounding headache, feeling more exhausted than I had the night before. The morning sun peeked through a crack in the drapes, and a lone bird chirped. I opened the bedroom door and saw Asher reading through my father's journal, the one that Papi had given to me after being shot by the Hastati. Full of his notes and discoveries, it had helped us find the spear the first time. I could only imagine that the other book he'd given me, the Guardian's Journal, held even more information. I could punch myself for having left it behind while I was escaping from the assassins who showed up at Simone's house. Who knew what kind of information was in there and who was now reading it?

"Good morning, Cassandra," Dame Elisabeth said, her eyes fixed on the laptop screen. "There are fresh strawberries in the kitchen, if you want to have that instead of the packaged meals."

"Strawberries?" We didn't have those when I went to bed.

"Yes, I got them earlier. They grow wild in the forest . . . down by the stream." She stopped typing for a moment and looked over at me. "I'll get some fresh food when I pick up your father, but you'll have to get used to eating the packaged meals. We may be here awhile."

I grabbed a strawberry and nibbled at it. "What time are we going to get him?" I asked.

Dame Elisabeth chuckled. "We? No, you're staying here."

"But I thought . . ."

"I already had this discussion with her," Asher muttered. "I don't like it, either."

"It's safer for you here." She turned back to face the screen. "I'll leave early this afternoon, and Asher will keep you company. I won't be away too long."

Asher waved me over and mouthed, "Come here."

"What's up?" I asked in a low voice, sitting down next to him. "Did you find something in there?" I pointed to my father's journal.

"Kind of." He flipped to a page toward the back of the book. "Look what your dad wrote in Spanish along the side of this page."

GJ—1610 fuego para abrir las puertas del destino. Pistas apuntan a la calavera del ángel que reside con las almas perdidas de Nápoles.

I reread what he had written, translating it for myself to English because that was the language I thought best in.

*GJ—1610 fire to open the doors of destiny. Clues point to the skull of the angel that resides with the lost souls of Naples.*

*"Fire to open the doors of destiny,"* I repeated. "What do you think it means? Is it some kind of instruction for how to use the spear?"

Asher shrugged. "I don't know. We can ask your dad when he gets here. But the GJ . . ." He leaned closer to me. "I think it refers to—"

"The Guardian's Journal," I finished his sentence. "Yeah, it must be. Do we know . . . Ow!" A sharp pain, like someone stabbing me behind the eyes, suddenly hit me. It was so intense that I felt like I might black out. I covered my eyes with the palms of my hands.

Asher touched my elbow. "Cassie? You okay?"

I couldn't speak. Flashes of light flooded my brain. Time seemed to slow down, and then I saw a snapshot from my vision. It was something that had whisked by so quickly that I had barely noticed it the first time. It was the same horrifying scene of Rome, with bodies decomposing in the familiar streets. But this time I zoomed in closer, until I was on my school's campus. I wanted to look away or close my eyes, but I couldn't. I tried focusing on the familiar surroundings: the fountain, the villa-like main building, or the iron gates . . . but it was the students' faces that I kept seeing. There was Gustav, the annoying boy from my history class who Simone always used to mock, lying still on the lawn. Next to him was Sandra, the quiet girl who had once lent me money for lunch.

I had somehow caused all of this. My use of the spear had created a future where my classmates were dying. I could feel my throat closing up. I was having a hard time breathing.

"Cassie!" Asher shouted, but his voice sounded so far away.

I tried to reply, but all that came out of my mouth was a guttural "uggghhh," and then the next thing I knew, cold water splashed on my face.

I coughed and pushed back my wet hair. "What? Why did you do that?"

Dame Elisabeth stood over me with an empty cup of water.

"You feel better, don't you?" she asked.

I nodded as drops of water rolled down my cheeks and onto my shirt. The pain had gone just as quickly as it had appeared. It was just like what had happened in the car except this one lasted much longer.

"What happened to you?" Asher asked, a concerned look on his face.

"I—I don't know. It was like I had the spear again, and I was seeing some of the same things."

"It's the echo tracing." Dame Elisabeth put the empty cup on the coffee table. "You'll need to find a way to work with it."

"Echo tracing? What is that?"

Dame Elisabeth handed me a blanket so I could dry my face. "You really don't know much, do you? I've got my work cut out for me." She sighed and sat beside me. "The visions from the spear leave a tremendous imprint in your brain. Humans only use a very small percentage of their mental capacity, and you are processing information that is very vast. What you've been exposed to will occasionally repeat, like an echo, as your brain tries to process it. You can use it to your advantage—it's a way to absorb more of it. The key is to observe more without letting yourself get lost within your own mind. To get out, you need to give yourself a reboot, as if you were a computer, so that your brain doesn't crash."

"A reboot? Like throwing water on me?"

"That or anything else that can shock your brain back into its normal function." Dame Elisabeth tapped my hand and stood. "You'll figure out something that works for you. It'll get better, and you'll adapt. For the time being, we'll keep an eye on you." She walked back to the kitchen table to continue doing whatever secret work she was doing.

"Don't worry," Asher said. "Now that I know, I won't let you get sucked into it again." He gave me a wink. "I'll always keep some water handy."

"Uh-huh," I muttered. Though he was trying to reassure me, this felt like yet another problem I'd have to deal with for the rest of my life. "I'm going to have some breakfast." I stood to get the strawberries but felt a little dizzy. I plopped back down on the sofa.

"Maybe you should just stay here," Asher suggested. "I'll get them for you."

I nodded, but I couldn't stop thinking about the "echo" I'd seen. Whatever horrible fate I had unleashed was going to affect the people I knew. And this wasn't some distant future. It would happen pretty soon. There was no way I could just sit by and let it happen. In fact, it might have already started.

# —SEVEN—

After breakfast, I spent some time rereading my father's journal and decided that I should add my own thoughts to the blank pages. I wrote about the visions, trying to describe everything in as much detail as I could. It was like a continuation of his research and it might help us sort through things later.

Once he got here.

In a few hours he'd want me to be his little girl again. And, although I was supposed to be this strong girl with the power to control the world's fate, at that moment that's what I wanted, too. If only for a minute, I wanted him to hold me in his arms like when I was young and tell me everything was going to be okay. It was almost like I needed him to fill me up with courage for what lay ahead.

I closed my eyes, thinking about all the times Papi had come to my room after I'd had a nightmare or when he'd stayed home from work when I was sick. Blood-related or not, he would always be my dad.

My thoughts drifted to one of my many memories of us visiting a museum. He had talked to me about the composition of the paintings. Wanted me to look at the balance of light and dark. Showed me how each painter treated the blank canvas differently. It was all about the artist's choices.

Choices.

That word again. What choices would I make, could I make, once I got the spear?

The sound of a car engine outside the cottage startled me. I jumped out of the chair where I had apparently fallen asleep and stumbled to the window. Dame Elisabeth was driving away.

I spun around.

Asher was gone, too.

My heart raced. How long had I been sleeping? Why didn't they wake me up? I rushed to the door and flung it open, ready to run after the car.

"Where are you going?" Asher asked, stepping out of the bathroom.

"Oh, um . . ." I slowly closed the door. "Nowhere."

Asher laughed. "You thought I left you here by yourself, didn't you?"

"No." I walked over to the kitchen and picked up the last strawberry. "And even if you did, it's not like I'd be scared or anything."

"Who said anything about being scared?" Asher leaned against the wall, a big smirk on his face.

"No one. I mean . . . I wouldn't be . . . ugh . . . you know what I mean." I took a bite out of the strawberry, a little of the juice dribbling down my chin. I swiped it away.

"Yeah, sure. You were just in a big hurry to get some fresh air. Uh-huh."

I glanced outside. This *was* the perfect chance to go and explore the area before someone said no. Why hadn't I thought of it before? This might be my only chance. "Yep, I need some fresh air. Figured I'd take a walk and get some more wood for the fire. You're welcome to join me if you like."

"That's not a good idea. Someone might see you."

"In the woods?" I rolled back my shoulders and opened the door. "I don't think so." I picked up Asher's pocketknife from the coffee table. "Coming?"

Asher's gaze bounced around the room. "Fine." He grabbed his backpack and slung it over his shoulder. "But we don't go far. The perimeter fence is set up about a kilometer away from here, so we stay close by. Deal?"

I couldn't keep the smile off my face. "Deal."

Outside, I felt exhilarated. There was a certain rush that came with the freedom. Not that any of it felt particularly dangerous. I knew the perimeter fence would warn us of anyone or anything that might come into the area. It made the nearby woods rather tranquil and peaceful. We wandered back past the woodpile, through the scattering of trees and thickets until we reached a clearing with a small stream running through it.

I thought about the riddle with the farmer, the wolf, the chicken, and the bag of chicken seed. Deciding to cheat a little, I asked Asher for help. He didn't really understand the riddle, so I explained it by using some of the things from inside his backpack.

"Okay, pretend this rope is the stream." I laid it out between us. "And I'm the farmer, and this pocketknife is the wolf." I picked up a rock. "This is the chicken, and the flashlight is the chicken seed. How do I get it over to your side of the stream if I can only carry one at a time?"

"Well, let's figure out the basic rule," Asher suggested.

"What do you mean?"

"The one thing that has to happen," Asher explained. "If we can figure that out, then we can work from there."

"Okay. So, the chicken can't be alone with the seed or the wolf because something will get eaten."

"Right. That means the wolf has to be alone or with the seed . . . no matter what."

"And the chicken has to be with farmer . . . always." The answer popped into my head. "That's it!"

"What is?"

"The chicken stays with the farmer."

Asher looked confused. "I don't get it."

"First, the farmer takes the chicken to the other side." I jumped over the rope and carried the rock over to Asher. This leaves the wolf and the seed together, which is what we said could happen."

"Uh-huh."

"Then the farmer comes back and picks up the wolf and takes him to the other side." I stepped over the rope and grabbed the pocketknife, bringing it back to Asher.

"But the wolf will eat the chicken when the farmer goes back for the seed."

"Not if the farmer takes the chicken back across the stream with him! Now the wolf is by himself, and the farmer goes back and drops off the chicken and takes the seed."

Asher began to nod. "I get it now. The farmer would drop off the seed with the wolf and on the final trip go back for the chicken that he'd left on the other side."

"Ha! We did it!" I grabbed the rock that had been our chicken and tossed it into the stream, watching it plunk into the water.

At the same time, I felt a rumbling under my feet. I looked around, confused. Had throwing the rock caused some sort of magical earthquake? Then I realized it wasn't the ground shaking, but the air around me. It was the sound of a helicopter approaching.

"Hide!" Asher yelled, shoving everything back in his backpack and racing out of the clearing.

I followed, thinking we were heading to the cottage, when he put out his arm to stop me and pulled me down behind some bushes.

"Don't move," he said.

The helicopter blades chopped the air right above us, but the canopy of trees kept us hidden from view. In the distance, I heard the faint sound of a siren going off. The perimeter fence had been triggered. Someone was coming.

"Do you think it's—"

Before I could finish my sentence, a large whooshing noise filled the air and something raced through the sky, rustling the leaves above us.

For a split second, everything grew still. And then it all exploded.

I felt the reverberation of the explosion in my chest as the sound wave pushed through the entire area. Smoke and dirt blasted through the air as a ball of fire shot up to the sky. The cottage blew apart into tiny bits, the force of the blast throwing fragments of wood and cement everywhere.

Asher and I covered our heads to shield ourselves from the raining debris, and I could feel myself shaking from the inside out.

I tried to process everything around me, but a loud ringing in my ears prevented me from hearing anything.

I watched Asher's lips move, not understanding what he was saying.

He pointed to the sky, where I saw two helicopters. One was red with white lettering on the side, and the other one looked like a military helicopter with weapons strapped all over.

I gasped. I couldn't believe what was happening. I wanted to say something, but the words wouldn't come out. Dumbfounded, I watched as the two helicopters swung around and started to head away.

"We have to go," I heard Asher say as the ringing in my head finally subsided.

"Where?" My heart was pounding hard against my chest. "We don't . . ."

My voice trailed off as two black cars sped down the dirt road, kicking up a cloud of dust, and stopped in front of what remained of the cottage. Then, from out of the haze, a man riding a motorcycle appeared.

My mouth went dry, and my hands began to tremble.

It was the Hastati assassin who had chased me and shot my father. He had found us!

"Her car isn't here!" a man shouted, stepping out of the black sedan. "We missed them."

I held my breath, not daring to make the slightest sound. Could we have caught a lucky break? Might they leave?

"Spread out and search the area," the Hastati assassin ordered as a bead of sweat ran down my side. "The old woman is tricky. They could be hiding somewhere."

"This way," Asher whispered and pointed toward the trees behind us. "Be really quiet but move fast."

I nodded, and we took off.

Thickets, branches, rocks, and trees . . . nothing slowed us.

I didn't have time to be scared or worried. All I focused on was getting as far away from the cottage as I could.

We stumbled across a narrow stream, and after what felt like an hour of plowing through the undergrowth, we finally found a small trail that made for a smoother run. We had stopped to catch our breath when we heard it.

A sound that made me quiver.

The rumbling noise of a motorcycle engine. The assassin had followed us into the woods.

"He's searching for us," Asher said, dropping to the ground and taking off his shoes and socks.

"What are you doing? We have to keep running."

"Making a weapon." He put a rock about the size of his fist into the sock and tied the bottom. "See?" He swung it around. "We can use it to protect ourselves." He handed me one of his sweaty, rock-in-a-sock weapons.

I shook my head and let him keep both socks. "That's not going to stop a gunman on a motorcycle." I took out the pocketknife. "I don't even think this will help. What we need is a motorcycle of our own."

Asher's head perked up. "You're right; we do." He glanced around. "There." He marched over to a small path.

"What are you doing?" I asked as he took out the rope and laid it down between two trees, covering it up with some leaves.

"Getting us that motorcycle." He tied one end about three feet up the trunk of the first tree. "We'll never make it out of here on foot anyway."

"But how are you going to get it?"

"Like this." He walked to the other end of the rope, and from behind the second tree, he pulled. The leaves went flying as the rope snapped up, creating a barrier. "Yesterday, you said you wanted to stop running and return fire. Well, this is where we start."

# —EIGHT—

The plan wasn't complicated. I had to lure the motorcyclist down the path. As he approached, Asher would pull the rope, knocking the assassin off the bike. Then we'd take the motorcycle and head back to Rome.

It was seriously crazy. But then everything that had happened to me in the last few days was already off-the-charts nuts.

"Ready?" Asher asked, hiding behind one of the trees.

I nodded.

I ran back toward a small clearing and pretended to be lost.

"Asher! Asher! Where are you?" I hated acting like a dumb girl who would give away her location, but it was all part of the plan.

The forest grew quiet. The assassin had shut off his engine and was now listening . . . trying to zero in on me.

"Asher!" I waited for the assassin to make his move. The seconds ticked by. Where was he?

My heartbeat quickened. I scanned the trees for any sign of movement. I could feel my hands become cold and clammy. It dawned on me that the assassin might not follow me on his motorcycle. Maybe he'd track me on foot. I could already be in his crosshairs, and he was taking aim at me.

The leaves behind me rustled.

I had to get out. Our plan had fallen apart.

I turned and ran back toward Asher. We'd have to figure out another way to escape.

That's when I heard the engine roar back to life. I glanced over my shoulder and saw a headlight shining between the trees.

The chase was on! This might actually work!

I took off, adrenaline making me surge ahead.

Behind me, I could hear the motorcycle getting closer. Branches were snapping. But I didn't dare look back. I continued running as fast as I could, right past Asher and into a thicket of trees and bushes, stopping to hide behind a large boulder.

The motorcyclist gunned the engine. That's when Asher pulled the rope taut, creating the barrier. Catching the assassin unawares, the rope knocked him off the motorcycle and sent the bike skidding into the bushes.

As soon as I heard the crash, I poked my head out. The motorcyclist was dragging himself over to where his gun had landed, but I got there first and kicked it away.

"Don't move!" Asher ordered, pointing his knife and holding his rock-in-sock in the other hand.

That's when I noticed the man's left leg, which stuck out at a strange angle, clearly broken. Had I seen this a few days ago, I might have been horrified. But now all I felt was relief. Relief that he wouldn't be able to chase after us.

The man remained on the ground. He looked like an animal that wanted nothing more than to pounce on its prey.

Asher took a few steps back. "You okay, Cassie?" he asked.

"Yeah." I lifted the motorcycle out of the bushes and saw that the front wheel was bent out of shape a little. I prayed that we'd still be able to use it. "Let's go."

"You won't get far." The man spoke with a heavy accent, and he grimaced as he tried to move.

"We'll get far enough." Asher walked over to me while keeping the knife trained on the assassin. He got on the bike and revved the engine.

"Tell your bosses I'm not the threat," I said, climbing onto the motorcycle behind Asher. "Sarah Bimington is the one they should be going after, not me. She has the spear, and if you kill me, then she'll be one step closer to having Tobias use it again."

"Not my concern," he answered. "And if the Hastati wanted you dead, then you wouldn't still be talking."

"What does that—"

Asher hit the gas, cutting off our conversation.

As we rode through the forest, Asher struggled to keep the motorcycle upright. I could tell that the bike wouldn't make it too far. We needed another way out. A few minutes later, I saw a hint of smoke in the sky.

"Asher!" I tapped him on the shoulder. "Asher!"

He slowed. "What?"

"Do you have any idea where we're going?"

He stopped and turned off the motor. "No."

"We need to come up with a plan. This motorcycle isn't going to make it much farther, and we need to figure out where to go."

Asher hit the kickstand, and we both slid off the motorcycle. "Agreed, but it's not like your grandmother knows where we are and is going to show up in some decked-out car to rescue us. You have any ideas?"

"Well, hiding out was obviously not a good plan. We just need to find a way back to Rome so we can tell Dame Elisabeth and my father what happened and locate Simone's mom." I walked up a small slope to get a better look at the area. "So what we need are directions back to Rome . . ."

"Cassie, stay out of sight. We took care of that motorcycle guy, but the other Hastati could be anywhere."

Ignoring him, I walked a little closer to a small clearing.

"Cassie!" Asher trotted up the slope to catch me. "Where are you going now?"

I pointed to the bit of smoke rising up over a line of trees. "There. I think that might be from a chimney."

"It could be a trap." Asher squinted as he stared through the trees. "The Hastati could already be there waiting for us."

"Fine. What do you suggest we do?"

Asher didn't have an answer.

"That's what I thought. C'mon, we can scope it out as we get a little closer."

I hurried along the edge of the clearing, trying to keep an eye on the smoke.

"And what do you expect to do once we get there?" Asher asked. "Assuming they even have a car, do you expect them to just give us a ride back to Rome?"

"No, but if it looks safe, then maybe we can use their phone and call my dad or Dame Elisabeth . . . see if they can meet us here. I mean, I know we don't have a number for them, but we can leave a message with the Knights of Malta."

Asher stopped walking.

I turned to see him standing there with his arms crossed. He didn't have to say anything else. I knew he was thinking that the phones at the compound were probably bugged.

"Okay, if not them, then who? Do you still have the number your uncle told you to call if something happened to him?"

"No. That and your dad's notebook were back at the cottage." Asher's shoulders slumped and he looked up at the sky. "We need to get someone that no one knows. That—"

"Gisak!" I blurted out. "Don't you know his number? We can call him. He can help us get back to Rome."

"I don't know." Asher rubbed the back of his neck. "He'll want something in return."

"We'll say it's on credit. That we'll pay him later," I persisted. "It's our best bet."

Asher nodded reluctantly. "Okay, I guess it can't hurt to check out the place and see about calling him."

We continued through the forest until we were only a small field away from the source of the smoke. It was a two-story villa, clearly someone's home. We hid behind some bushes for a while, watching for any activity. At one point, someone set a pie by an open window, but nothing else happened for a long time. It was getting late, and we weren't any closer to leaving.

"That's it." I leapt up and headed toward the clearing. "We need to see if they have a phone."

Asher grabbed me from behind and carried me back under the canopy of trees. "Are you crazy?" he asked. "Or do you have some sort of a death wish?"

"The Hastati aren't there. It's obviously some family's house. We need to get moving."

Asher took a deep breath. "Fine," he sighed. "I'll go see if they have a phone, but you stay hidden behind these trees, just in case. If I don't come back in ten minutes, you take the motorcycle and go."

"I'm not going to leave you."

"Cassie, you don't have a choice."

Asher didn't get it . . . There was always a choice. But I wasn't going to argue with him. "Whatever you say," I replied, plunking myself down behind a bush that kept me hidden from view but still let me catch a glimpse of the villa.

"Good." Asher gave me an approving nod. "I'll be right back."

He crossed the small field and approached the house. First, he peered through a side window and then went to the front door. As he lifted his hand to knock, the door opened. A middle-aged man stood there with a woman hovering behind him. They were too far away for me to hear what was being said, but the man nodded and motioned for Asher to come inside.

Asher glanced back in my direction, then entered the villa.

There was nothing left for me to do except wait. I listened to the sound of the wind through the trees. Felt the dry earth beneath my feet. Watched a trail of ants search for their own hidden treasure.

I looked at the villa again.

Had it been ten minutes? I didn't have a watch, but it certainly felt like it.

I cracked my knuckles.

I grabbed a lock of my hair and wound it nervously through my fingers. What if Asher was in trouble and needed to be rescued? Maybe I should go over and peek through the windows. But if I did sneak over and there wasn't a problem, I'd mess things up. Plus, who knew if it had been ten minutes.

I was still arguing with myself when the door opened again. Asher waved at the woman and started walking back toward the forest.

He passed by the bush where I was hiding and, without looking at me, said, "Don't get up. Wait two minutes before you come meet me. They might be watching."

Before I could ask any questions he disappeared farther into the forest.

This time I counted to 120, then made my way in the direction he'd gone. My heart pounded, and suddenly, I felt very small among all the trees. I tried to quiet my breathing so I could hear any twig snapping or leaf rustling.

"Asher?" I whispered, searching the dim forest. All I saw were tree trunks, closing in around me.

I took a few more steps, the dried leaves on the ground crunching beneath my feet.

"Asher?" I whispered again and waited.

"Yeah?"

I spun around as he popped out from a tree right behind me.

"What was that all about? Are you trying to freak me out?"

Grinning, he walked around the motorcycle he had brought over. My immediate instinct was to wipe the smirk off his face, so I gave him a shove. "You want to fill me in on what happened?"

"Didn't mean to worry you." He strolled over to a broken log, straddled it, and sat down. He opened up his backpack and tossed me a water bottle. "Got you this."

I gulped down the water, suddenly realizing how thirsty I'd been.

"So what happened?"

"I called Gisak. He's on his way, but it'll still take him an hour or two to get here. He's going to meet us just down the road from the villa."

"Two hours!"

"It's the best he can do, and at least it'll be dark by then."

"Yeah, I guess." I didn't like the idea of staying in one place for so long, but at least we now had a plan. "We should keep the motorcycle next to us, just in case."

"I was thinking the same thing."

I took a seat next to him on the log. "So what was up with making me wait two minutes before coming back here?"

"It was my cover story. I said my friends and I had been camping and our car broke down. Told them I needed to call my uncle and then head back to the campsite because my friends were waiting for me. Wouldn't make sense if they happened to watch me go into the woods and see me talking with a girl, right?"

"No, guess not." I tucked my knees under my chin. "So we just wait?"

"Pretty much."

"You think the Hastati are searching the forest for us?"

"I don't know. I thought for sure they would've sent back that helicopter to look for us."

"Guess we got lucky."

"Maybe, but I think something else is going on." Asher grabbed a stick and started sharpening the end with his pocketknife. "We just haven't figured out what it is."

We stayed quiet for a few minutes, Asher drawing squiggles in the dirt with the stick he'd fashioned into a spear.

I folded my arms on top of my knees and rested my head on them. But I stayed on high alert, my entire body ready to make a run for it, if needed.

Soon the last bits of light drifted away in the western sky. It would become pitch black in a matter of minutes.

"Come on," Asher said. "Gisak should be there by now, and it'll be hard for someone to spot us now that the sun has gone down." He reached down a hand and helped me to my feet. We walked along the road, leaving the motorcycle hidden in the forest. The half-moon gave enough light that we could see the dirt road that lay about three hundred feet in front of us. Behind us, in the distance, I could see a small light coming from the villa where Asher had made the call.

"Let's see where he is." Asher pulled out his flashlight and flicked it on and off a couple of times.

Headlights down the road turned on and off.

It was Gisak.

We ran toward the car, Asher several strides ahead of me.

Even in the darkness, I could see Gisak's silhouette as he opened the driver's side door and stepped out.

"Jump in the back," Gisak called out, motioning us both over as we approached. "You can tell me what's happening when we get out of here."

Asher froze, and I ran right into him.

"What—?" But then I saw why Asher had stopped so abruptly.

My eyes widened with fear.

The car's passenger door had opened, and someone was getting out.

Gisak was not alone.

# —NINE—

It only took a moment for me to recognize Gisak's passenger: Simone. My traitorous, former best friend.

Anger replaced fear.

I couldn't believe it! How dare she show her face again?

Simone stood behind the car door, unsure of what to do next.

I marched straight toward her, not even thinking of the fact that her mother might be there, too. "What are you doing here?" I yelled.

Asher grabbed me by the arm, stopping me a few feet away from Simone. "Gisak, do you know what you've done?" he said, pulling me back. "Who you brought here?"

"What?" Gisak looked at Simone, then at us, clearly confused. "Is she not your friend? She said you got separated and that you'd eventually call. That I was supposed to bring her with me."

"She betrayed us and played you!" Asher eyed the tree line. We would have to make a run for it and hope to find the busted motorcycle. "This is a trap!"

"No, it's not." Simone moved away from the car. "I swear." She took a step toward us, and we took three steps back. "You have to believe me. I thought my mother was going to help. I thought it was the only way . . . but I was wrong."

"We don't believe you," I snapped. "You're a liar!"

"I am not someone who gets played," Gisak announced, circling around the car and forcing Simone to move toward the side of the road. "I don't know what happened between the three of you, and I honestly don't care. Asher . . . do you want to leave her here?"

"Yes!" we both answered.

"Cassie, please. PLEASE," Simone begged. "No one knows I'm here. I came because I want to help. Because I know how badly I messed up. I would never do anything to hurt you."

I glared at her. "But you already did. You lied and stole . . ." I paused, realizing that Gisak was listening to everything we were saying. "You know what you did."

"I thought it was the right thing to do." She inched closer to me. "My mother said it was the best way to protect you. That she'd make sure you were safe." Simone took a deep breath. "But that was a lie . . . I know that now. I should've talked to you. We're a team, and I should've trusted that."

"What kind of trouble have you gotten into, Asher?" Gisak asked. "Maybe I can help."

"No, that's okay. I got this," Asher answered, pulling Simone and me a little farther away from the car so Gisak would be less likely to hear us. "Just give us a minute!" he shouted as Gisak got into the car. "Listen, Simone," Asher whispered. "What do you want? For things to go back like they were? Well, they can't."

Simone ignored him. "Cassie, you know me better than

anyone in the world. You and your dad are the closest I've ever been to having a real family. The way we shared secrets, how I felt when I got to spend the holidays with you, when you borrowed my clothes . . . it was like we were sisters. I only wanted to protect you. You have to believe me."

Her words were slicing through my rage. Those things had all been real. I knew Simone cared about me. But . . .

"Why are you even listening to her?" Asher scanned the area. "She's a deceitful, conniving, little menace, and she's put us in danger again."

"No, you don't understand." Simone glanced back at Gisak and lowered her voice. "The danger is my mother. She's . . . she's coming after you. I came here to warn you."

"Okay, you did that," Asher said. "Now you can go."

"Cassie, please. I know that you have every right not to trust me, but I swear I only want to help. I'll do whatever you say." She reached into her cross-body purse and pulled something out. "Here."

"What could you possibly have that Cassie wants?" Asher asked.

"Unless it's the spear," I said, "it won't make a difference."

"I couldn't get the spear, but I got this. It's the journal," Simone explained. "The one that you left back at my house when we ran out." She paused. "The Guardian's Journal. My mother had it. I took it . . . to give to you."

Asher and I exchanged a look, and Asher quickly reached for it. He flipped through the book, barely seeing the pages in the glow of the moonlight. He took out his flashlight and inspected it further. "It is the Guardian's Journal," he said in awe.

I couldn't believe we had it back. When I'd left it at Simone's house during the shooting, I thought for sure the Hastati had taken it. I eyed Simone. There was still a chance that this was some sort of mind game or trap. I couldn't let my guard down. "Why the sudden turnaround?"

"I overheard my mother talking," Simone said bitterly. "She's not who I thought she was."

"Neither are you," I answered.

"But I betrayed you because I thought I was helping you." Simone shook her head. "My mother . . . she . . . she doesn't care about anything or anyone. She only wants more power and control. She even has that crazy guy, Tobias, with her. They've teamed up, but when she realized that he couldn't use the spear anymore, she went ballistic. Cassie . . . she figured out that you must have touched the spear and become bound to it."

Asher's head snapped up from reading the journal.

"No, she's wrong," I said quickly, my heart beating a little faster. "I didn't—"

"She knows, Cassie," Simone interrupted. "I know. Don't even bother denying it." Simone shook her head. "I wish you would've trusted me enough to tell me, but, in retrospect, I guess it was a good thing I didn't know."

I stayed quiet, only taking a moment to look at Asher. I couldn't believe that my secret was out. Dame Elisabeth, the Hastati, Sarah Bimington, Tobias . . . even Simone . . . they all knew I was bound.

"The important thing is that I heard her say that she should've had Dante take care of you at the hospital. She told Tobias not to worry because she'd fix it so he could control destiny again. That's why I know she'll stop at nothing to find you."

"So you think she wants me dead?" I swallowed the lump in my throat. "Your mother really wants to kill me?" Simone's mother was always travelling, so I'd never met her until this week, but I'd been in her house a bunch of times. Simone and I had had sleepovers there and baked brownies in the kitchen. I couldn't believe this woman would be willing to kill me.

Simone nodded, tears streaming down her face. "All she cares about is power, and Tobias will give that to her. She never cared about me or protecting you. I wish I'd never given her the spear. That I could take it all back. Maybe if the Hastati had gotten it, everything would've worked out. I don't know." She wiped her cheeks. I'd never seen Simone cry before. "Haven't you ever done something wrong but, at the time, you thought it was for the right reason?"

I thought of how I had used the spear to save my father—only I'd saved the wrong father. And by doing that, I'd brought Tobias back to life and put the entire world in jeopardy.

Yeah, I understood what she meant.

"Do you know where the spear is?" I asked, my voice not as harsh.

"I think so." Simone dabbed at her nose with the cuff of her sleeve. "I'm almost sure my mother took it to our house just outside Positano. I think it's in her safe."

"Cassie!" Asher looked up from the journal. "You can't be serious. You're not thinking about trusting her again?" He pulled me closer to him. "This could be a trap."

"If it were a trap, I would've brought my mother here," Simone argued. "I ran away from her to help you."

I wanted to trust Simone. She had been my best friend, and I didn't want to think she'd purposefully put me in danger. Plus, I needed to find the spear, and she might be the best way to get it. "Your place in Positano . . . does it have a room with curved windows that face the sea?" I asked, wondering if my vision of Tobias had taken place in Simone's house.

"Yeah. Several."

"And it's up high on a mountain or something? Not down on the beach or anything," I continued.

"It's up on a cliff. An outcropping that kind of sticks out from the mainland." Simone scrunched her eyebrows. "What's going on? Why the questions?"

"I think I may have seen it before."

"Well, sure, maybe. Back in Rome, there's a picture of my mom and me taken at that house. It was in a silver frame in the living room. Maybe that's where you saw it."

"Uh-huh," I muttered, but that wasn't what I was talking about.

"Cassie, are you thinking . . . ?" Asher didn't finish his question, but I knew he understood. My vision confirmed what Simone said: Tobias and the spear were at Simone's mother's house.

I nodded. "It has to be."

"Has to be what?" Simone looked baffled.

"We need to go there," I said, ignoring her.

"No, you can't," Simone said, panic in her voice. "My mother will kill you if you go there."

"Getting the spear is the only solution," I said, turning to Asher to hatch my plan. "And we can catch her by surprise. Go to her before she comes to us."

"Yeah, I figured you might say that. Let's see if we can get a ride there." Asher walked over to Gisak, with Simone and me following right behind him. "Gisak, I've got another favor to ask. Instead of Rome, will you drive us to Positano?"

"To get the spear?" Gisak's lips curled into a smile. "Absolutely. Get in."

The three of us froze.

"What?" Asher could barely contain his shock. "No, I don't know what—"

Gisak scoffed. "Please, Asher . . . give me a little more credit. I know all about the Hastati and the Spear of Destiny. Did you think that you were the only one using the tunnel between my shop and the monastery?"

Asher's eyes widened. "You've been spying on me?"

"I deal in information," Gisak explained. "I like to know what's going on. Don't worry, your uncle and I arrived at an understanding of sorts . . . You have nothing to fear from me. I'll keep your secret."

I inched closer to Asher. Now I didn't know if we should trust Gisak and go with him.

Asher was apparently thinking it over as well.

"I don't think you have many options," Gisak said. "I've known for a while and haven't betrayed you." He glanced at Simone. "Unlike some people, apparently."

We were in the middle of the forest, and our options weren't very promising. The longer we stayed, the more likely it would be that the Hastati would find us.

"Okay, yeah." Asher opened the rear door of the car and motioned for me to get in.

Simone hesitated. "What about me?" She looked at each of us. "I'm going, too, right? I can help get you into the house. There's a lot of security, but I can bypass it." Getting no response, she added, "Please, Cassie. Let me prove myself to you. I can even try to find out when my mother isn't home."

It was true we might need her help, but more important, I wanted to give her a second chance. A second chance to make things right. Just like I was getting.

"Yes, you can come," I said.

Simone threw out her arms to hug me, but I took a step back. I wasn't ready to forgive her . . . only to give her a chance.

"No way." Asher looked at me like I had completely lost my mind. "We can do this without her."

"It'll be better with her," I argued. "I think she can help us."

"I can. I really can." Simone's voice had an upbeat sound to it.

"This is not a good idea." Asher took a deep breath and slowly let it out. "All right, get in . . . but we're still watching you. And we'll have Gisak kick you out of the car if anything weird is going on."

"I'll prove myself to all of you. You'll see." Simone turned around to look at me sitting next to Asher in the backseat. "And I'll never let you down again, Cassie. Never."

# —TEN—

Gisak quickly got us out of the forest and onto a main highway. As we drove through the night, Asher flicked on the small car light and paged through the Guardian's Journal. After an hour, I couldn't wait any longer.

I leaned against Asher. "My turn. Let me see it," I said in a low voice.

He held up a finger. "In a minute. I'm working on something."

Simone turned around. "I flipped through it earlier, and most of it looks like gibberish," she said. "You're not missing much."

"Uh-huh," I muttered. I certainly wasn't going to tell her that my father had made reference to the Guardian's Journal and something about a fire and an angel's skull. There were clues in there; Simone just didn't know it.

The car slowed down as we pulled into a truck stop.

"What's going on?" I asked. "Why are we here?"

"Refueling before we head down to Positano. First us, and then the car," Gisak said, parking the car next to a large pickup filled with old, beaten-up furniture.

Stepping inside the small restaurant, we bypassed the convenience store and headed straight to the counter where hot, ready-made meals were served. My stomach growled as I caught a whiff of garlic and onions. I narrowed down my choices to either the spaghetti Bolognese or the risotto. Truth be told, I was hungry enough to have both.

"Order what you like," Gisak said, standing behind me. "I will pay."

"Why don't we each order something different and then share?" Simone suggested.

It was something we always used to do, but I didn't want her to think things could go back to normal so easily.

I shook my head. *"Il risotto, per favore,"* I said to the girl behind the counter. She served me a plate of food, placed it on an orange tray, and slid it down to make room for the next order. Not waiting for Simone, I picked up my tray and headed to one of the small tables by the window.

I was thinking about my father and wondering how we could contact him, when Simone placed a water bottle in front of me. "Thought you might want this." She was standing in front of me holding a salad and diet soda. "Um . . . is it okay if I sit with you?"

I shrugged and took a bite of my risotto.

Simone pulled out a chair and sat down. "Cassie, you know that if I could go back and change things, I would. The whole thing was . . ." Simone stopped speaking as an old man walked past our table and headed outside.

I didn't want to talk to her, so I focused on the old man, who went to his pickup truck and rearranged some of the furniture piled up in the flatbed.

"It was a mistake. I thought I was protecting you," Simone continued. "I didn't know that it was putting you in more danger."

"Mm-hm." I now faked interest in the latest soccer highlights being shown on the large TV in the corner.

Simone took a sip of her soda. "If Asher hadn't been so hardheaded, then maybe I—"

"Stop right there," I said. Simone was not going to pawn off any blame. This was all on her. "You are no one to criticize."

"No, I just meant that . . ." She pushed the lettuce leaves around with her plastic fork. "I don't know. Things could've been different. You're my best friend, and if we would've talked things out more without him being involved, then maybe I wouldn't have felt like I needed to—"

"To what?" I challenged her, my voice rising a bit. I leaned across the table and whispered, "To completely betray me and go against what I specifically told you not to do? Asher has been the one by my side in all of this, so don't think even for a second that what you did has anything to do with him. You made your own choice."

"I know," Simone mumbled. "I know."

Asher put down his plate of pasta. "Everything all right over here?" he asked, sitting down next to Simone. He had a concerned look on his face.

"Fine," I said through clenched teeth.

"Uh-huh." Simone nodded without looking up.

A minute later, Gisak strolled over to the table, carrying a small brown bag.

"You're not eating?" Asher asked him.

"Later. I'm going to get gas while you finish in here," he answered. "Don't take long."

"Not a big talker, that guy," Simone muttered.

I was about to respond when something on the TV caught my eye.

The risotto I had just eaten suddenly felt like it might come up again. Luckily, all that came out was a barely audible "Oh, no."

Asher and Simone turned to follow my gaze.

There on the screen blazed the Italian words for "armed and dangerous" beneath a picture of Asher. The report went on to show the monastery cordoned off with yellow police tape and a policeman speaking to the camera. A school picture of me flashed on the screen, labeling me an accomplice to Brother Gregorio's murder, with the phone number to a tip line.

Had Simone's mom called in a fake tip? Or was it the Hastati? Either way, now the entire country would be on the hunt for us.

"We need to go. Right now." Asher kept his head down as he quickly made his way to the door.

I glanced over to the girl behind the counter. She was on the phone and facing the TV. Had she noticed us? Was she already calling the tip line? I hurried outside and was about to dart across the parking lot toward the gas pumps when Asher stuck his arm out, stopping me midstride.

"Wait. Look." Asher pointed over to Gisak, who was arguing with a gas station attendant. "Something's up over there."

I strained to hear what Gisak and the attendant were saying to each other, but even though the night was relatively quiet, I couldn't hear them.

What if the attendant was accusing Gisak of helping criminals and he'd already called the police? Or what if Gisak had seen the TV report himself and decided that the reward money was better than helping us? Either way the result would be the same . . . and we were trapped out here in the middle of nowhere.

"They're talking about us!" Simone's panicked tone matched the adrenaline pumping through my veins. "We have to get out of here! The police or worse, my mother, could have this place surrounded in minutes."

A rumbling noise filled the air. The truck filled with junk was leaving.

"Follow me," I said, running toward the pickup as it pulled out of the nearby parking space.

Asher shook his head. "But we should—"

The rest of Asher's comment was lost to me as I scrambled into the flatbed, pushing aside some trash bags to make room for the three of us. Simone scrambled in right after me.

"I go wherever you do," Simone said to me with a meek smile that was so unlike the Simone I knew.

I ignored her and gestured for Asher to come join us.

The truck was rolling along the dirt road, and thanks to a mattress draped over the rear window and the bumpiness of the road, the driver had no clue that he had just picked up some stowaways.

I waved to Asher to hurry up. He finally moved ... racing over and, with one leap, bounding into the back of the truck.

"I don't know about this," he muttered as the truck stopped for a moment before turning onto the main highway. "We don't even know where he's going."

"We'll get off at the first city ... wherever that is," I answered as we all scrunched down to avoid being seen by any passing car. "At least we got out of there. We can take a train or bus whenever he stops."

As the truck picked up speed, it became harder and harder to talk without raising our voices. Every time we tried to say something, it was like we were in a wind tunnel, so eventually we just stayed quiet.

The highway was pretty solitary. Only occasionally would a car zip past us, its headlights slicing through the darkness before the night swallowed us up again. We were in what my dad would call in Spanish, *la boca de un lobo* ... a wolf's mouth. A dark and dangerous place. I looked up at the star-filled sky, and my thoughts drifted to my dad. I wondered if he knew we'd escaped or if he thought we'd been captured or killed by the explosion. If only there was a way I could somehow reach out to him and let him know I was fine.

When we'd been taken under Dame Elisabeth's protection, I thought we'd be safe until we decided on the best plan, but now things were spiraling out of control. We were separated from my dad and grandmother. Simone had found us, and no matter how much I wanted to trust her again, I couldn't help worrying that I'd let a traitor into our midst. Plus, we were now wanted fugitives.

If only I had the spear, I could choose what would happen next. Control the immediate future. It would be so much simpler.

But that was a fantasy. I wasn't completely sure how to use the spear without creating a bigger mess in the long term. Every action had consequences.

Without realizing it, my eyes closed. A strange sensation washed over me, and it felt like I was caught between being awake and dreaming. I could still feel the bumps in the road, the wind whooshing past my ears, and the chill in the air, but I couldn't move. Pressure built in my head, like a headache, but much sharper and centered right above my eyebrows.

Along with the pain a familiar image formed—one I'd witnessed briefly when I'd used the spear, then again in an earlier echo tracing: a man—Tobias?—looking out a window toward a brilliant blue sea. But this time the image didn't float away. I felt like I was diving into a photograph.

I focused on the room. Tobias stood by an arched window overlooking the sea, and there was a large bed a few feet away. I tried turning my head to see more of the room and anyone else who might be in it, but my vision only let me see the room from one angle. I noticed a large gold mirror hanging on the wall across from me. I stared at it, allowing my eyes to focus on the image being reflected. Asher was across the room closing a closet door and—

A pain shot across my cheek as a hand smacked me... hard.

"Ow!" My eyes popped open, and I scrambled to get away from the shadowy figure hovering over me. A soothing hand touched my shoulder.

"Cassie, you're okay now!" I heard Simone shout, right next to my ear.

I realized I was in the truck, and we were still driving down the highway. I placed my hand over my stinging cheek. "Who slapped me?" I called out.

"I'm sorry," Asher said. "It was the only way I could snap you out of it."

"You were moaning and wouldn't wake up," Simone said. "What happened? Does it have to do with the spear?"

I stayed quiet. She might know that I was bound to the spear, but I wasn't going to tell her that I'd actually changed the future and was now having "echo tracings" of the vision I'd experienced.

"Don't worry about why it happens," Asher said. "But if you ever see Cassie go still like that, you do whatever it takes to snap her out of it."

"Preferably, something that doesn't hurt," I added, rubbing at my still-throbbing cheek.

"What happens if no one is around and it happens again?" Simone asked.

"Nothing good," Asher responded. "Nothing good."

# —ELEVEN—

Eventually, the truck began to slow. I leaned over the side and saw we were approaching a small town. I could see a supermarket up ahead.

"Should we jump out?" Simone asked.

"Not yet." Asher slipped his backpack over his shoulders. "But we should get ready to do it before he parks."

A car approached. Its headlights got closer.

"Duck down," Asher ordered. "Don't let them see you."

I curled up on the floor of the truck, Simone's head right next to mine.

"We can look for a train station once we get out," Simone said. "I brought money with me."

"Uh-huh." I nodded.

"Or we can try to get a hotel room for the night and head out in the morning," she said. "Whatever you think is best."

The car went around us as the truck briefly stopped to turn onto a residential street.

Asher sat up. "Let's go!"

"Now? We're still moving." I glanced around as we slowly passed some apartment buildings.

"Just bend your knees and roll when you hit the ground."

"Can't we just wait until he stops again?" Simone asked. "I'll break a leg if I jump."

"We're getting farther away from the city center and—"

The pickup slowed down to almost a crawl as it pulled into a long driveway.

"Now!" Asher leapt over the back of the truck's tailgate and hit the ground running.

Simone and I stepped over it, balancing on the rear bumper before dropping down to the ground. We both stumbled onto our knees but quickly popped up and ran toward Asher.

The three of us made our way back to the main part of the dark and mostly desolate city. We stayed in the shadows, even though it seemed like the entire town's population had gone to bed.

"Do you think we're headed toward the train station?" I asked after we'd walked around aimlessly for a while. "Maybe we're going in the wrong direction or the town doesn't even have one."

Asher jumped on top of a bench and then leapt like a cat to the top of a small brick wall. His body silhouetted by the moonlight, he walked along, balancing on the wall to try to get a better view. At the end of the block, he dropped back down to street level to meet us.

"Do you think jumping around on top of walls like some sort of bad-movie ninja is a good idea?" Simone said. "I thought we were trying to be inconspicuous."

"It's called reconnaissance, and I was careful."

"Uh-huh." Simone rolled her eyes.

"See anything?" I asked, trying to ignore their obvious dislike of each other.

"No, it's too dark, and there are too many buildings around," he answered. "We should keep moving."

"If Gisak is being questioned, can we really trust him not to say anything?" Simone whispered as she walked alongside me.

"Look who's asking," Asher answered with disgust dripping from every syllable.

"Ugh." Simone glared at him. "Look who's asking," she repeated, mimicking him exactly.

"I don't sound like that, by the way," Asher said as matter-of-factly as he could to Simone. "Your impression of me is way off."

"I don't sound like that by the way," Simone said, copying his voice once again with her unusual talent of impersonating people. "Your impression of me is way off."

"Stop it," Asher warned, but Simone seemed to take his frustration as an invitation to do it again.

"What . . . you don't like the sound of your own voice?" she asked, feigning innocence while still speaking like him. "Imagine how we feel hearing you."

"Enough." I spun around like a mother scolding her children. "This isn't helping anything. We're tired and lost. Let's just keep walking until we bump into a sign or something that points us to a bus or train station."

"Psst," a hushed voice called out from a doorway across the street. *"Bambini."*

We froze.

A figure stepped out of the doorway—a nun wearing a blue dress and habit.

*"Vengano,"* she said, waving us over.

I pulled back, deeper into the shadow of the building beside me.

"Psst," the nun called out again.

"Should we go over?" Simone asked. "I mean, she can probably point us toward the train station."

"Yeah, but what if she recognizes us?" Asher whispered.

"So, we aren't going to ask anyone how to get out of here?" Simone shook her head. "If we keep walking around, we might end up running into the police."

"But even a nun might turn us in if she thinks we're criminals," I argued.

"Fine, then what if I go? My face wasn't on TV. You two can stay here."

Asher and I looked at each other. Clearly, neither of us loved the idea of trusting Simone with our safety.

"Come on," Simone huffed. "You'll be watching me the whole time, and I'm speaking to a nun."

"Fine." I nodded. "Just find out about the train station and come right back."

Simone smiled and hurried across the street.

I watched her talking to the sister. The conversation grew lengthy. It had to be about much more than just getting directions.

Simone looked over her shoulder and pointed to us.

Asher and I took a couple of steps back, withdrawing further into the night.

Had I made a mistake in trusting Simone? What if Asher was right about her?

The nun nodded, reached into her pocket, and gave something to Simone. As she ran back to us, the nun went back into the building and closed the door.

"What was that all about?" I asked as Simone approached.

"Train station is closed. She said they start again in the morning, but that we can spend the night in the church."

"I don't know . . ." I didn't trust anyone at this point. Not a nun. Not Simone.

"What did she give you?" Asher asked, suspicion in his voice as well.

"Huh?" Simone looked down at her hand. "Oh, it's the key to the side chapel door. She thinks we're runaways. Told me she once lived on the streets and it's not safe. Said that Naples is even more dangerous."

"Naples?" I didn't understand why she'd mention that city.

"Yeah." Simone nodded. "I asked about a train to Positano, but she said the train only goes as far as Naples. That we'd have to take a boat or a bus the rest of the way."

"You told her where we were headed?" Asher exclaimed. "How stupid are you?"

I couldn't believe she'd given away so much information, either.

"How else was I supposed to find out about the trains?"

Simone argued. "I've only gone to Positano by either boat or helicopter. Plus, she thinks we're runaways. It's fine."

"Whatever," Asher said dismissively. He gazed over Simone's shoulder to the small church. "We do need a place for the night, and she never saw our faces."

"You'd actually stay there?" I asked incredulously. "What if she turns us in because we're runaways?"

"I don't think she will," Simone said. "She seemed like she really wanted to help."

"It's better than waiting at the train station or on the street, where the police might see us," Asher replied.

I didn't like it. There was too much at stake. But then again, what else could we do at this time of night.

"Aghhh." I gripped the sides of my head in pain. I was being sucked back into another echo tracing of my vision, but this time, I was going to fight it. I couldn't slip into that trancelike state . . . there was too much to do.

My body shook involuntarily, and I felt myself start to laugh as hands tickled the sides of my torso. The pain vanished, and I saw relief in Simone's face.

"Better than a slap, right?" Simone arched an eyebrow. "Good thing I know where you're ticklish."

I nodded, unable to speak. Exhaustion weighed me down like someone had draped a lead blanket over me.

"Cassie, you're not looking that great," Asher noted.

"Gee, thanks," I muttered.

"Such a gentleman," Simone added.

"I mean she looks tired. We should all get some rest," Asher explained. "We have a long day ahead of us tomorrow."

I nodded, still a bit dazed by the echo tracing. Then, with Simone and Asher on either side of me giving me some support, we crossed the street and headed inside the church.

Shadows bathed the interior. The only light came from the flickering candles on either side of the altar. I lay down in the third pew from the back. Far enough away not to be seen if anyone were to peer into the chapel, but close enough to the door that I could make a quick escape if necessary.

Simone sat in the pew right in front of me, while Asher took the one behind me. In seconds, the chapel became still once again with only the sounds of my own breathing reaching my ears.

"Cassie." Simone broke the peaceful silence. "Thank you for giving me another chance."

"Uh-huh," I muttered, exhaustion slowly creeping up on me.

"And don't worry," she said. "Between the three of us, we'll figure out a way to get rid of that power so you don't fall into any more of those trances and you can be normal again."

I said nothing. Simone didn't understand that it was much too late for that. I had set things in motion, and from now on, I was the only one who could stop them. The power was part of me.

There was nothing normal about me anymore.

# —TWELVE—

"Cassie. Cassie." Someone shook my arm. "It's time to go."

I opened my eyes, and for a split second, I thought I was seeing an angel. I blinked and realized it was Asher, his head framed by the glow of blue, red, and yellow light coming in through the stained-glass windows behind him.

"Simone. Where is she?" I said, my voice a bit hoarse as I sat up.

"I'm ready," she answered from the chapel doors, which were cracked open, allowing the morning light to sneak inside. "Just keeping an eye out for anyone who might come over."

"Why didn't you wake me up earlier?" I slipped on my shoes. "I don't need to be coddled."

"Not doing that." Asher walked down the center aisle. "You needed to rest, and it's still early. We've got a big day ahead of us."

"The nun is coming back!" Simone announced. "Pretend to be asleep."

Asher darted to one of the pews, and I lay back down. I heard the door open, and by peering underneath the pews I could see the sensible black shoes of the nun standing in the doorway.

Simone spoke to her in hushed tones, but I could make out something about friends sleeping. I caught snippets of what the nun said. She offered to keep the chapel doors open every night and bring us food. She wanted to make sure we were safe because the streets were no place for kids. Simone thanked her but said we'd be fine once we got to our friends in Naples.

There was a little more chatter, which I couldn't hear because a car engine roared outside.

Simone closed the door. "All clear," she called out.

I stood up and saw her holding a basket. "What's in there?" I asked.

Simone removed the small towel that was draped over the top. "She brought us some bread, cheese, and fruit to eat."

"Why?" Asher popped up and walked to the door, opened it a little, and peered outside. "I mean, why is she doing all of this instead of turning us in 'for our own good'?"

Simone shrugged. "She's young, maybe only about ten years older than us. I think she just wants us to be safe. She offered to leave the chapel open at night."

"I heard her say something about that." I reached into the basket and pulled out a piece of bread.

Asher glanced over at us. "Well, we're not staying."

"Obviously," Simone answered. "But at least we have food. And she told me the train station is only about five blocks from here. Just make a left outside and then a right at the second corner."

"Then let's go," I said. "We might be able to catch the first train of the day. You said you had money for the tickets, right?"

Simone nodded and tapped her purse. "I took care of that before running away. My mother always has extra cash lying around."

Asher pulled the door open, allowing the morning light to stream in. "Okay, let's get out of here."

We darted outside, and in less than thirty minutes we were at the station boarding the 7:05 train to Naples.

We chose one of the empty train cars toward the back and settled in for the two-hour trip. As we stopped in other towns, more passengers got on, but no one seemed to take any notice of us. I kept my head turned to the window, Asher had his nose buried in the Guardian's Journal, and Simone closed her eyes to nap.

As we got closer to Naples, I noticed Asher jotting down some things on a piece of paper. Then I heard him gasp.

I tapped him on the knee. "What did you find?" I asked. "Something that can help us?"

"You're not going to believe this." Asher looked at Simone, whose eyes remained closed. He lowered his voice a little more and leaned closer to me. "I was going page by page, so it's taken me a while to go through it, especially since different Guardians write in their own native languages, but then I found this." He could barely mask his excitement as he pointed to a page written in red, yellow, and black and covered in swirls of ink, so it was hard to even make out some of the letters. On two of the corners were small symbols like crosshairs.

"It looks like a long chain of random letters," I said.

"Uh-huh. Now look at what's written before that." He tapped the left side of the journal. "It's dated 1610. It's written in English by a Guardian who is concerned with what is being chosen for the future. He believes that nothing should be predetermined because God intended for there to be free will, so fate shouldn't be controlled by anyone. Look what he says here." Asher put his finger on the bottom paragraph.

*I have discovered a way to open the doors of destiny, allowing all possibilities to exist and for free will to once again roar like a fire. It will not be contained and will spread like a great blaze. Nothing will be certain . . . neither good nor evil.*

My heart skipped a beat. It reminded me of the words my father had written in his journal. I had thought my father's clue was referring to a way to use the spear to determine destiny . . . but this Guardian was writing about not having a preplanned future at all. Maybe that's what my father had meant, too. I could almost feel everything shifting. There might be a way out that wouldn't involve me having to choose what would happen in the future.

"Do you think it's true?" My voice quivered. "I mean, could we undo it all?"

"This Guardian seems to think so. Look at the very last line. I think he's even telling us how to do it." Asher read aloud: *"To release the fire of free will, the first sparks of knowledge are seen through the flame."*

"Yeah, but what do you think it means, though?" Simone asked, one eye now open.

"You were awake?" Asher frowned and sat back in his seat.

"Come on," Simone complained. "If I'm going to help, I think—"

"We don't need your help," Asher retorted. "Other than getting us into the house, there's nothing we need from you."

Simone glanced over at me, expecting me to defend her. I looked away.

"Okay, I get it," she said. "I know neither of you trust me, but I can help. I'm the one who got you the journal . . . remember?"

I considered what she was saying. She already knew I was bound to the spear. What was the point of excluding her from this? She might be able to help.

Nudging Asher's knee, I said, "Let's hear her out. Simone has good ideas. Sometimes."

A faint smile of satisfaction crossed Simone's face. "I was thinking that we should get a match and—"

"Burn the page?" Asher interrupted. "Are you crazy?"

"No, not burn it," she responded indignantly. "I'm not crazy."

"We look at it through the flame," I said, realizing what she meant.

"Exactly!" Simone said. "Cassie gets it."

"Maybe . . ." Asher hesitated, stared at Simone, and then shook his head. "No. Remember what your dad wrote?"

"There's more you don't know, Simone," I explained. "We think my dad had been trying to work on this clue already."

Asher recited the note from my father's journal from memory: *"Fire to open the doors of destiny. Clues point to the skull of the angel that resides with the lost souls of Naples."*

"Right." I nodded. "So, it sounds like the flame is hidden with skulls . . . or something. And I don't think it's an ordinary flame, either."

"An angel's skull?" Simone's eyes lit up. She loved all sorts of spooky things. She used to beg me to go on ghost tours of Rome with her, which I never did. "That's so . . . awesome."

"Yeah, well, things aren't always what they seem," Asher replied. "And I can't imagine it's an actual skull, let alone an angel's skull."

"So maybe we should still try a match." Simone reached across the aisle toward Asher's backpack. "Don't you have one in there?"

"No," Asher said, blocking the bag with his legs. He turned to another page in the journal and continued reading.

We all stayed quiet for a few moments. I kept thinking about how this could change everything. There was now another way to fix things. To release destiny. If it really worked.

"Oh, boy." Asher looked up at us. "Now I really don't think the match idea of yours is right. The next entry in the journal . . . it isn't very long, but it's written in 1842. It talks about the flame having been lost and a secret group searching for it." He turned the book around to face me. "Read it."

I looked at the words. "I can't," I said. "I don't know French."

"I do." Simone peered over my shoulder and looked at the page. "Wow!" she exclaimed. "It seems like they really were able to do something about freeing destiny."

"Why?" I asked. "What does it say?"

She paused to read a little more. "This guy writes that the Hastati decided to use the spear again and there were unintended consequences, but they couldn't undo them. He says that since they no longer have the flame, the way to release destiny has been lost." Simone glanced up at me and Asher. "I guess they couldn't just use a regular fire. But what kind of flame lasts for centuries?"

Asher shook his head and shrugged. "It doesn't make sense to me, either."

Simone went back to reading. "It ends with the writer praying that their luck changes or that the Fates choose to help them." She flipped the page. "That's it. He doesn't write anything else. I don't think they ever found it."

"So let's say it's some special type of fire and we figure out what it is, then what?" I asked. "We just stare into it and hope that something gets revealed?"

Asher slumped back in his seat. "I don't know."

I sighed, realizing that the way to release destiny depended on finding a fire that had probably been extinguished centuries ago. We were grasping at a dream. The idea that there could be a way to release destiny was too good to be true.

It looked like I was back to having to choose the fate of the world. It was my responsibility, and I would do what I had to do. If only I knew what choices to make.

# —THIRTEEN—

The train began to slow down as we approached Naples, the last stop on the main line, but we were nowhere near ready to get off.

"Shouldn't we try to find the angel skull that your dad mentioned?" Asher was insisting. "He said it was in Naples, and we're here anyway. If it can help us figure out how to release destiny so that no one controls it anymore, then—"

"No," I answered for what felt like the tenth time. "What's the point in finding out how to free destiny when we don't have the spear?" My jaw clenched at having to explain what seemed so obvious to me. "Plus, think about what you're saying. An angel skull? Some long-lost fire? Those all sound like wild-goose chases. We need to focus on getting the spear, because once I have it, then I can change the future. That's something we know can happen. Go for the sure thing."

Simone scrunched her eyebrows. "Why do you want to change the future?"

Asher and I exchanged a quick glance. Simone didn't know about the chain of events I'd created. She had no clue about the path I'd put the world on.

"Neither of you is going to tell me?" Simone asked after a couple of moments of silence. "Okay, maybe you'll trust me later, but I do agree with Cassie. Getting the spear gives us the biggest bargaining chip, and Cassie can always use the spear to get out of any jam."

"So we all agree?" I stared at Asher until he gave me a slight nod. "Good, we stick to my plan," I said. "Get out of the train station, and head to the port. Once we find a boat, we sail down the coastline past Positano to Simone's house."

"Shouldn't we dock somewhere near Simone's house and sneak in through a servants' entrance or something?" Asher suggested.

"I already told you that it's not that type of house. Let me draw it." Simone grabbed a newspaper that had been left on one of the seats and pulled a pen from her purse. "It looks like this." She drew little waves around what looked like a small mountain with a house built on the edge. "It's connected to the mainland by some jagged rocks, but the house is at the very top of the outcropping, and there are sheer drops of about three hundred feet on each side. That's why my mom had it built there. She usually comes and goes by helicopter. No one gets in by land unless you're a professional rock climber."

"In that case, I can get in," Asher stated with a cocky attitude.

"Uh-uh," I said. "You're not going without me. We have to find a way for me to get in with you."

"Right, so back to my idea." Simone drew a small semicircle at the bottom of the cliff she'd drawn. "There's a sea cave on this side of the outcropping. Mother had a staircase built into it that takes you right up to a door in the kitchen. It's how boat deliveries are usually made." She tapped the newspaper. "If we can get a small boat, we can go through there."

"So it's basically what I said at the beginning," Asher said. "We use the servants' entrance."

"No, it's . . ." Simone paused for a moment. "Fine . . . maybe it is. Does it matter? We can still get in that way."

"But won't they see us coming by boat?" I pointed out the obvious. "I mean, there has to be security, right? Won't they try to stop us?"

"I'll tell them we have permission."

"You think they're going to listen to you?" Asher shook his head. "This isn't a good plan."

"It *is* a good plan!" Simone argued. "You haven't heard all of it yet." I could tell she was trying to come up with ideas as she went along. "The guards do whatever my mother says without question and if I can get her to call . . . and . . . and . . ."

The train's brakes squealed as we entered the station. Simone stuck the newspaper under her seat.

"She can tell them to follow your orders," I said, the entire plan falling into place in my head. "They just have to hear it from her."

"What?" Asher looked at me as if I was crazy. "You expect her mother to—"

"YES!" Simone exclaimed. "That's perfect."

"We can't contact Simone's mother. That's suicide."

"Who said anything about contacting her, my dear," Simone said in a voice identical to her mother's. "I will give the orders by phone, and they'll obey."

I nodded. She could imitate her mother and have the guards do what we wanted. We'd be able to search the house and get the spear. I'd be able to change the future. The thought of having the spear sent a shiver of excitement through my body.

The train finally reached the platform, and the three of us got out. The Naples station buzzed with people hurrying off the train cars while others ran to catch them. We avoided making eye contact with anyone wandering around the platforms . . . afraid someone might recognize us from TV—or worse: that actual Hastati might be patrolling the area. We headed out, trying to mix in with the throng of passengers rushing to the glass doors of the main terminal's exit.

"Wait." Simone stopped a few feet in front of the tourist information desk. "Before we go out there . . . I need to get some things." She took off toward a small kiosk without saying anything else.

"What is she doing?" Asher whispered.

"Don't know." I quickly turned my back on a security guard who was walking toward us and pretended to study a map of the metro stations. I noticed a display of travel brochures and grabbed a small map of the city as the guard sauntered away down the corridor behind us.

A few minutes later, Simone returned holding a paper bag. She had already wrapped a brown plaid scarf around her neck.

"Seriously?" Asher said incredulously. "You went shopping?"

"No." She pulled out a cap with a Juventus soccer team logo on it and thrust it into his chest. "I got us disguises."

Opening the bag, I saw several sunglasses, hats, and a couple of scarves. It was perfect.

"I'm more of an AC Milan fan," Asher mumbled, putting on the cap and pulling the brim down low. "But this'll do."

"Thanks, Simone," I said, putting on a blue cap with the word *ITALIA* written in big letters. "It was a smart thing to get."

You would have thought I'd given her a million dollars. She flashed a smile and gave me a big hug as we headed to the station's main exit.

Stepping through the glass doors, we were greeted with the noise and congestion of Naples and a line of white taxis three cars deep.

I looked down at the small map I had picked up. The port was at least a thirty- to sixty-minute walk from where we were.

"Cab?" Simone asked.

I slipped on the sunglasses and nodded. It would be better to take our chances with one random taxi driver than wander the streets of a city we didn't know.

Asher waved over one of the taxis, and the three of us climbed in the backseat, making sure we didn't let the driver get a good look at our faces.

*"Al porto per favore,"* Asher told the driver, directing him to the port.

*"Quale?"* he replied, shifting gears and rolling out of the line of parked cabs.

"Which one?" I looked at the small map I had picked up. There was a large port and then a couple of smaller ones, but none were labeled.

"*Il principale,*" Simone answered quickly and vaguely. *The main port.* "We can figure out where to go after he drops us off there," she whispered to me.

"*Calata Porta di Massa?*" the driver asked, giving us the specific name of a port.

"*Sì,*" I replied, figuring that was as good as any.

Simone and Asher relaxed back into the seats as the taxi blended in with the city traffic. The sounds of the city were muffled by the glass and an Italian ballad playing on the radio.

But I could feel my adrenaline building. We were close to getting the spear back. I could feel it in my bones. Even though I was still afraid of making the wrong choice, there was a growing sense inside me that when the time came, I'd be able to figure out the right thing to do. Something about having the power to control the future made me feel strong and fearless.

It felt good.

It felt right.

Perhaps Dame Elisabeth had a point, and this was my calling, my destiny. Maybe I could be the one to make everything better.

Didn't I owe it to myself, and to the world, to at least find out?

# —FOURTEEN—

The sun was shining brightly against the cloudless blue sky. It was a perfect excuse for the three of us to keep our sunglasses on, and it gave me a little more security that we wouldn't be recognized.

The song on the radio had been replaced by a more upbeat tune, and the cabdriver was now drumming along on the steering wheel. Everything seemed to be going fine until a radio call from the dispatcher announced a reminder.

"All drivers, police have asked that you be on the lookout for two young teens, a fifteen-year-old male and twelve-year-old female, wanted in the death of a monk in Rome," the dispatcher announced in Italian. "Report any suspicious passengers to the authorities."

The three of us tensed.

My eyes caught the driver looking at the three of us through the rearview mirror. He had stopped drumming along with the song, but was now humming his own tune as he made a quick right.

I checked the name of the street we were on, Via Duomo, against my map. We were headed away from the port. Something was wrong.

"We have to get out," I whispered to Asher. "He suspects something."

*"Ferma l'auto!"* Asher demanded.

The driver glanced back, and Simone quickly pretended she was about to throw up.

*"Ferma l'auto!"* Asher ordered again.

The driver pulled over to the side. *"Esci! Esci!"* He shouted for Simone to get out, as the last thing he wanted was for her to get sick in his car.

Simone passed me a ten-euro bill and stumbled over to the corner.

I handed the driver the money and quickly followed Asher out of the car. We stood near the alleyway, pretending to comfort Simone. The cab slowly peeled away from the curb.

"Is he gone?" Simone asked, her hands still on her knees.

"Yeah." I smiled as the cab continued down the street. "That was quick thinking."

"Well, I figured that no one likes puke in their car, and I've faked enough barf attacks at school to be convincing." Simone chuckled to herself. "Cassie, do you remember the time in Latchke's class with—"

"With the beef stew from your thermos?" I giggled, remembering the shocked expression our teacher had at finding the mess next to his desk. "Remember I told him I had to go—"

"To take care of me! We ended up watching TV instead of taking that pop quiz." Simone sighed. "That was awesome."

It had been. It also felt like it was a very long time ago.

"Um, I hate to cut short this stroll down memory lane," Asher interrupted. "But we should get out of here. We're not in the clear yet. That driver could still report us."

"Yeah, you're right." I opened up the map and pointed to a few of the side streets that led to the harbor. "We can go this way. Maybe go to this smaller marina over here. Just in case he tells someone that we were headed to the main port."

"Okay, let's go." Simone adjusted her sunglasses and covered her hair with the scarf.

We had walked about a block and were waiting with a small crowd of people at a crosswalk when I spotted our taxi driver speaking to a couple of police officers. He was directing the officers to the place where he'd dropped us off.

My pulse quickened. "Oh, no," I muttered.

"What?" Simone glanced around.

I motioned to the opposite corner. "I think he's reporting us to the cops."

"Stick with this crowd," Asher said as the light changed and everyone began crossing the street. "They haven't seen us yet."

The people walking alongside us gave us cover until we reached the other side. We darted around the first corner we saw . . . Unfortunately, it was a dead-end street.

"Now what?" Simone asked.

"Stay here a second." Asher peeked back around the corner. "One of them is walking this way. We need to go quickly."

Just as I was about to move, I felt my feet become heavy, as if I was wearing fifty-pound shoes. The world around me started to spin, and I could feel my knees buckling.

*No . . . not now,* I thought.

"Cassie!" Asher scooped me up in his arms before I crumbled to the floor. I felt him carry me behind a large dumpster as I slipped into another echo tracing.

This time the image was of me on a motorboat in the middle of the sea. I couldn't tell where I was, but the boat was anchored and in the distance there was a storm edging closer. Lightning lit up the sky between the dark clouds. I wanted to turn and head to shore, but it felt like I was stuck staring out at the horizon, forced to watch the tempest that would soon overtake my position. In this small snippet of time, I couldn't even turn to see who was with me, but I knew I wasn't alone . . . yet it certainly felt like I was isolated.

I concentrated, trying to force my mind to retrieve something more useful from my vision than this solitary moment.

A hard pinch on my arm made my eyes flutter open.

"Cassie, good. You're back. We need to get out of here." Simone was pulling me up. "I'll help you walk."

I struggled to stand. I hated the feeling of being weak and fragile after an echo tracing. Then I noticed that something was wrong. "Wait, where's Asher?"

Simone scowled. "He's gone."

"What?" I must've not understood what she said.

"The cop . . . he was coming this way, and you were out

of it." Simone put her arm under mine for support and helped me get moving. "So Asher took off, hoping that the officer would chase him and he'd buy us some time."

"Why would you let him do that?" I complained even though I knew it was futile at this point. "We're supposed to stick together. I need him in order to use the spear."

"Yeah, well, I didn't think it was a good idea, either, but it seemed to work."

I gathered up my strength and trudged to the corner, peeking out at the busy road. "How does he expect us to find him in this place?"

Simone shrugged. "He said he'd find us. To just get you away from this street and go to that small marina on the map."

I had the same feeling as in the echo tracing. I was with people, but still felt like I was in this mess by myself. I'd be facing the storm alone. And maybe that was the way it was always supposed to be. "With or without him, I'm going to get the spear," I muttered. "I'm too close to let anything stop me."

Simone gave me a strange look.

I realized how that sounded. "You know what I mean . . . we've come too far not to finish things. We have to get the spear away from your mom in order to make things right again."

"Yeah, I know. It just didn't sound like you."

I shrugged off her comment. "Okay, so . . ." I pulled out the map, not wanting to waste any more time. "Up ahead . . .

we can take Via dei Tribunali, then cut back down this other street that leads toward the water."

"You feel up to walking that far?" Simone asked, her eyes still showing some concern.

"Yeah." I nodded, my mind more focused than ever on changing the future. "I'll stop to catch my breath if I have to, but I don't want to waste any more time."

All I wanted was to get to the spear. Once I had it, everything would work out. I could make things right again. It was part of my destiny and I was learning to accept it.

# —FIFTEEN—

Via dei Tribunali turned out to be a narrow pedestrian street with shops on either side, and there were enough people walking around that we blended into the crowds. The stone buildings seemed to get older with each passing block, and when we reached a series of arches in front of a building with crumbling columns, I stopped to check the map once more.

"Cassie, look . . . that skull."

"Huh?"

Simone pointed to a sign hanging from scaffolding across the street. A small church was being restored, and there, on the banner over the front door, was a picture of a skull with angel wings on either side.

"*Chiesa di Santa Maria delle Anime del Purgatorio ad Arco,*" Simone read out loud. "That picture has what looks like an angel's skull on it, and the church has the words Souls of Purgatory in the title . . . Isn't that kinda what your dad wrote about? Lost souls and stuff?"

"Yeah," I said. She was right, but I didn't have the energy to get excited about anything other than the spear. I just wanted to get to the port. "We can come back later. After we get the spear."

"But we're already here." Simone tugged on my hand and pulled me closer to the church entrance. "I have a hunch. We should at least take a look. See what's inside."

"Simone . . ." But my protests fell on deaf ears. Simone was already passing a small stone pillar with a brass skull on it and going into the church. I followed her inside, noticing a small sign by the main door stating that tours were given every hour on the hour. I made a mental note that we were not going to stick around for any tour, no matter how much Simone begged. We'd be here for five minutes . . . tops.

As Simone wandered around the nearly empty church, I stayed close to the entrance. From my vantage point, the space looked like so many other beautiful but small Italian churches. It was ornate with marble and gold leaf decorating the walls and painted archways highlighting statues. There were pews lined up toward the front of the church, where a large Renaissance-style painting loomed large above a small altar. A painted cupola allowed natural light into the building. It was full of grandeur and opulence, not what one expected to see among the small shops and apartments that lined the street outside.

"Psst." Simone motioned for me to join her as a young woman wearing a blue blazer and khaki pants handed her a flyer and walked away.

I hurried over, hoping that Simone had gotten her fill of the place so we could go.

"So, did you find it?" I asked, looking around for the picture of the angel's skull that we'd seen outside, but not seeing it. "Can we get going?"

"Look behind the altar, underneath the painting."

My eyes shifted over and there it was: the stucco of the

skull with wings. Still, it didn't shed any light on how we would discover the special fire that was described in the Guardian's Journal.

"Perfect. Now we know where it is," I said, trying to get us back on track. "Once we find Asher and get the spear, we can come and look to see if there's a reference to a fire or something."

"That's just it." Simone smiled. "According to what that tour guide told me . . . I think the answer is right under our feet."

I looked down at the marble floor.

"No, not the floor." Simone arched a single eyebrow. "A mirror church underneath us."

"A what?"

"It's an exact copy of this building, built underground for the dead. She offered to give us a tour in about twenty minutes, but I paid her a little extra to let us go down there and explore on our own now."

"Simone, we can do all this later after we find Asher and the spear."

"But this place closes early . . . We might not get another chance. Come on." Simone pulled my arm. "It won't take long. If there's nothing there, we leave."

We entered a dark passageway and descended a stone staircase. A light flickered above us as we exited onto a balcony overlooking the underground church.

A slight gasp escaped my lips as I gazed down below.

It was an eerie replica of the church above us . . . minus

any of the decorations, marble columns, or artwork. There were no pews and no altar. The walls here were stripped bare, not even covered with a single coat of paint, and the entire place was dimly lit. On the far wall, there was a large black cross and nothing else. It looked like something out of a movie. A scary movie.

"This place is so incredibly awesome," Simone whispered, rushing down the stairs to explore the area.

I hesitated. It felt like we were dropping down into another world. A place of death.

"C'mon, Cassie," Simone called out, her voice reverberating through the empty room.

As much as Simone seemed to be enjoying this, I hated it. This was not where I wanted to be. I watched as Simone disappeared through an archway, leaving me by myself up on the balcony. But being alone in a place like this was far worse than exploring with Simone.

I raced down the steps to find her.

Once at the bottom, I looked around the cavernous church. Without pews or an altar, the place seemed less like a church and more like an empty shell.

"Simone?" My voice echoed eerily in the space. "Where are you? We need to go."

"Here," she answered, sounding upbeat. She really did like all this stuff. "Wait till you see this."

I reluctantly trudged toward her voice. I found her in a room off to the side of the main church. "Can we go? I don't . . ." I stopped talking as my eyes adjusted to the dim lighting. The place was full of skulls and bones. They were stacked in cubbyholes along the wall and on the floor. "Whoa . . . are all these real?"

Simone nodded. "The tour guide upstairs says they used to bury bodies down here and that people pray for the souls that might be in purgatory." She gestured at the flowers and notes that were tucked in among the bones. "See, they leave things for the dead. Isn't it freaky cool?"

I glanced around at all the bones, my skin crawling with goose bumps. "Okay, but there isn't a fire that can release destiny in here, so let's go." I rubbed my arms. "You know I don't like this stuff."

"Are you looking for something?" a raspy voice asked from the far corner of the room.

A woman with long, gray hair stepped out of the shadows. She was wearing a black dress, and I noticed that there was a chair next to a stone pillar where she must have been sitting.

"We were just leaving," I replied, not wanting to intrude on whatever she had been doing.

"You speak English," Simone noted, taking a step closer to her. "Can you tell us a little more about this place?"

The old woman looked at the entrance behind me. "You came alone? No tour guide?"

"She said we could look around on our own," Simone answered.

"Mm-hm." The old woman stared past Simone and focused on me. "And you? Are you also interested in learning more?"

There was something about this woman that gave me the sensation that she either knew us or knew what we were doing. Or maybe I had seen a glimpse of her in the echo tracing. I wasn't sure.

"Well?" The old woman had an irritated tone in her voice.

Simone nudged me, so I gave a small nod.

"All right." She motioned for us to follow her back to the far end of the room, where we were surrounded by more skulls and bones. She pointed to them. "Here, in this place, alliances are formed. The living pray for lost souls with the hope that once those souls reach salvation, they will return the favor and help those that prayed for them. It's a way to keep the fire burning."

"Fire?" I asked. "Did you say fire?"

The old woman smiled. "I did. The fire of faith, but that's not the one you seek . . . is it?"

Simone and I exchanged a quick glance. *Did this woman know about the fire that was referenced in the Guardian's Journal?*

"You would be surprised at how much I see and hear. No one seems to notice when I come and go." She sat down in the chair, and from a basket on the floor, she pulled out a pair of shiny scissors. Ignoring us, she began to cut small strings from a large embroidered cloth.

"Um, this fire that we're looking for," I said. "Do you know where we can find it?"

She didn't look up. "Depends."

"Depends on what?" Simone asked.

The old woman kept snipping away at the strings. "On whether you have the correct answer." She put down the scissors and showed us the embroidered cloth she had been working on.

I drew closer to read the words written in gold thread.

*From dawn to dusk we rise and grow,*
*Our scheduled destiny we always know,*
*To disappear into the night*
*Or choose a candle for the light.*
*We follow, mimic, or sit as stone*
*Fated to never call one our own.*

"It's a riddle," Simone whispered.

"I know." I reread the words. "I think it might be the sun," I said to Simone.

"You have a guess?" the old woman asked. "You only get one chance."

"Not yet," Simone answered, then got close to my ear. "Look." She pointed to the second half of the riddle. "The last lines don't make sense if the answer is the sun. It's got to be something else."

"Time is up." The old woman took back the cloth, folded it, and stuffed it into the basket along with the scissors. "What is your answer?"

I couldn't think of what it could be. A person or thing that grows during the day, disappears at night, and copies another.

"Can we each get a guess?" Simone asked, trying to stall.

"No." The woman picked up the basket and stared at me.

"And who exactly are you?" Simone continued talking while I kept thinking. "I mean, how do you have what we're looking for?"

"I'm Aisa, and I've had it for a long time. But that's enough questions." I could hear her foot tapping under her long skirt. She was growing impatient. "Do you have an answer for me?"

"Um . . . I . . ."

The old woman turned her back on us. "You are no different. Your understanding is still cloaked."

Cloaked. I looked at the dark corner behind the old woman. An answer hidden in the shadows. That was it.

"Shadow!" I shouted. "The answer is a shadow. It grows during the day, disappears at night, copies whatever the object does, and can never have one of its own."

The old woman turned, a pleased look on her face. "Finally," she muttered. She reached into her basket and gave me something wrapped in blue velvet. "Perhaps my sisters were right. You do have potential."

"Sisters?" Simone asked.

The old woman shifted her gaze to Simone. "You . . . well, they're not too fond of you," she lamented. "Never a second chance for a first impression, but I believe in redemption."

I eagerly tore aside the blue velvet. When the cloth fell away, it revealed a glass paperweight. Not exactly what I expected. "I don't understand. What is this?"

"The fire. Once you are out of the shadows, and in the light, you will see the flame. Just remember to use it to see what is unseen."

"Is that another riddle that—"

Voices carried into the room. Simone and I spun around, quickly realizing that a tour was being given in the main part of the underground church and that they would likely be coming in here to see the skulls and bones.

"You must go," the old woman urged us to leave. "They will be coming in here soon."

"But . . ." Simone wanted to ask more questions.

"*Mi seguano.*" The tour guide was already telling the tourists to follow her.

"This place is too small . . . someone might recognize me," I said to Simone. "I have to go."

Simone knew I was right and followed me as we made our way past the tour group, up the stairs, and into the well-lit upper church.

"What exactly did she give you?" Simone asked, looking around to make sure we were alone.

"I'm not sure." I pulled out the glass object. It was in the shape of a leaf. It had swirls of red, yellow, and orange in the middle and, along the edges, the glass was tinted a dark green.

"Looks like a Murano glass paperweight."

I held it up, and as I did it caught the sunlight, causing the center to sparkle and glow.

Simone bounced up and down. "Cassie! That looks like—"

"A flame!" I exclaimed, still staring at it. "I know." I put my eye to the glass to see if it made things look different. I turned to the angel's skull behind the altar to see if some secret knowledge would be revealed to me . . . but nothing happened. It was like looking through any other piece of tinted glass.

"It's got to be the key to the code written in the Guardian's Journal, right?" Simone was almost giddy with excitement. "We can use it to end all of this. That piece of glass might allow us to read what was written in the journal. Kinda like my match idea. You could go back to normal and not have to worry about choosing the future."

"I guess so." I slipped the "flame" into my jacket.

Simone scrunched her eyebrows together. "You don't sound too thrilled."

"I am. It's just . . ." I cradled the glass ornament inside my pocket, then gave it a squeeze. "We don't know what this all really means or if this thing will actually help us free destiny. Getting the spear has to still be our first concern. For now, we need to keep our focus and hope Asher finds us."

Simone snorted. "Yeah, sure, but can you imagine Asher's face when we tell him what we found? He's not going to believe it."

I gave her a halfhearted smile, but I was now starting to worry about how this might affect things. If this was the key to releasing destiny, should we use it? Perhaps that wasn't a good idea. How long had it been since destiny was truly free? There were some really bad people in the world, and they shouldn't be allowed to shape our future. By using the spear I might be able to stop them. Become a real hero.

In fact, the more I thought about it, releasing destiny might be the worst idea of all.

# —SIXTEEN—

We had finished walking down a long path of stairs that took us straight to the water's edge, and still there was no Asher. I had assumed he'd wait for us somewhere along the way, but the fact that we were already by the marina made me worry.

"Do you think the cops got him?" Simone asked as we gazed out at all the boats.

"I don't know." I moved closer to the side of a nearby hotel, away from the outdoor cafés that lined the street. "If they did, we're going to have to find a way to get him out."

"Let me check something." Simone squeezed into a narrow gap between two buildings and pulled out her wallet. "I have about seven hundred euros total," she said, counting her money. "Is that enough for bail?"

"If he's been arrested, they're not going to let him out at all. He's wanted for the death of his uncle." If only Asher hadn't taken off, we'd be on our way already. "We're going to have to break him out somehow," I said, thinking of the different scenarios we might face.

"Or we could get the spear without him," Simone suggested.

"We can't. He's the only one who can get me out of the Realm of Possibilities and—"

"The Realm of what?" Simone interrupted.

I hesitated, but at this point it didn't seem like it mattered much if she knew. "It's kind of where my mind goes when I touch the spear. Asher is the only one who can bring me out of it," I explained. "That's why we need him. It's weird, I know."

"Not weirder than anything else that's happened." Simone tapped her fingers against the wall. "Okay, what if . . . What if you don't touch it? We go get it, just the two of us. Like we did with the flame. I could be the one to handle it and—"

*Plink.*

Simone looked over her shoulder to see what had made the noise. No one was there.

"You heard something, right?" she asked.

I nodded. The space between the buildings was so small. It must have been an animal. Probably a rat.

*Plink.*

This time, I saw a small pebble bounce off the ground.

My eyes shifted up to see who or what was making it rain down rocks.

Asher waved at us from the rooftop of the five-story building.

Before I could do or say anything, he motioned for us to stay put and then disappeared from the edge.

"He has a flair for the dramatic, doesn't he?" Simone muttered, leaning against the wall. "I'm surprised he didn't get himself caught by the police on purpose just so he could do a cool escape."

"Mm-hm." I bit my bottom lip. I was glad that Asher was back, but Simone was right; he did go over the top a bit with the whole jumping off rooftops thing. He wasn't invincible, even though that's the way he acted. He seemed to forget that I was the one who had the power to control the future.

A couple of minutes later, Asher joined us.

"I found us a boat," he announced. "But we need to go quickly because I think the cops might still be looking for us."

"Sure, but first . . ." Simone pointed to the left pocket of my jacket. "Want to tell him?"

"What?" Asher looked at me, then Simone, then back at me. "Did something happen?"

I glanced at the people passing by. "Why don't we talk about this once we get going?"

"Just tell me quick," Asher said.

"We found the angel's skull in this church for lost souls," Simone blurted out. "It was awesome."

Asher's eyes widened with surprise. "The one Cassie's father wrote about? Are you sure?"

"Uh, yeah." Simone smiled smugly. "We even had an encounter with a mysterious old woman who gave us the flame."

"Is this true, Cassie?"

I nodded. "It's not a real flame, just a glass paperweight that looks like one. It might decipher the code the Guardian wrote." I looked around. "I'll show you once we get the boat."

"Okay, that'll be safer." Asher pointed to the far corner of the marina. "There's a man over there who'll rent me a boat for two hundred euros a day."

"You have two hundred euros?" Simone raised a single eyebrow. She knew that he didn't.

"No, but you do," Asher retorted.

"True." She flicked her wrist and brushed him aside. "But just remember that you needed me for this. And that I am helping."

Asher grimaced. "I have a feeling she's not going to let me forget."

# —SEVENTEEN—

We cut through the waves in our small motorboat for a couple of minutes, the city of Naples growing smaller and smaller as we headed down the coast toward Positano. Our plan was simple: We'd get off in Positano and Simone would call her house and get the guards to leave. Once they were gone, we'd head over and do a quick in-and-out type of mission to get the spear. At that point, I'd use the spear to find a path where my classmates and people all over the world didn't die and Asher would make sure I didn't get stuck in the Realm of Possibilities. It seemed like a good plan.

Asher shut off the engine and anchored the small motorboat in the middle of the sea with the shoreline still in sight. "I think we're far enough away. Let me see the flame."

I pulled out the tinted glass paperweight. "Here," I said, handing it to him. "Let's not spend too much time out here though. We can always see what it does after we get the spear."

"This won't take long." Asher passed me his backpack while studying the paperweight. He held it up to the light, flipped it over, and even looked through it.

"We did all that, too," Simone said. "Although we have a theory of what it's supposed to do."

Asher looked at me. "What is it?"

It seemed like the quickest way to get Asher focused on the spear was to spend a few minutes with the idea of releasing destiny. "I'll show you, but I don't think it's going to work." I unzipped the backpack, took out the journal, and turned to the coded page with its different-colored letters.

"Let me have the glass," I said, balancing the journal on my lap.

Asher handed it to me, and I slid it over the notebook as though the page were a magical Ouija board that would convey its deep, dark secret to us. Some of the letters disappeared and reappeared, depending on where I placed the glass. Yet nothing seemed to be revealed.

"Anything?" Simone asked, hovering over me.

"No, I told you this was a long shot," I answered, unsure if I was happy or sad that it wasn't working.

"Hold on." Asher put his hand on mine to prevent me from moving it. "Look." He rotated the glass so that each tip of the flame lined up with the crosshairs on the corners of the page.

"Good call!" Simone shouted. She squinted at the page, and her face fell.

Over half of the letters had disappeared under a swirl of the matching color, but what was left behind was still a bunch of random letters. I rolled my eyes. Sometimes I hated being right.

"I thought that was it," Simone muttered.

"It still might be," Asher said. "It could be a code within a code. Do you have a pen and paper with you?"

"Yeah." She opened her purse and gave him a slip of paper with a pen. "It's a receipt, but you can use the back."

Asher looked at the front and raised his eyebrows. "Four hundred Euros for a pair of boots?"

Simone shrugged. "I like nice things."

"There are a lot of letters left," I said, wanting to get started. The wind shifted and the boat began to rock back and forth, making it more difficult to keep the paperweight completely aligned with the crosshairs. "Ready?"

"Go," Asher said, the pen poised to write.

I called out all the letters:

*YTWJQ JFXJIJXYNSDGFHPYTYMJBTWQIYMJWJFQR RZXYGJUJWRFSJSYQDKNQQ JIGDMFANSLYMJTSJBMT JSYJWXINJNSXJQKQ JXXXFHWNKNHJBMNQ JNSXNIJY MJWJFQR*

Asher stared at what he'd written on the receipt. "It could be some type of substitution code, but it might take me a while to figure out."

"It looks like a storm is coming," Simone said, pointing out to sea, where gray clouds were rolling in. "We should get going."

Asher glanced at the horizon. "Those clouds will probably blow away," he said, returning his gaze to the letters. "We're fine." He then looked up at Simone again. "Are you seasick or something?"

"No . . . I'm just not a big fan of being in a tiny boat in open water when there's a storm nearby."

"Simone's right. We should head to Positano and set things up so we can get the spear," I said. "We need to stay focused." I had a feeling that Asher could lose track of time with the code, and as much as he wanted to find a way to release destiny, it was more important for us to get the spear away from Sarah Bimington.

"I am focused." Asher was making chains of letters on the receipt and crossing them out every time something didn't work out. "We're getting closer to figuring out how destiny can be freed. This is as important as getting the spear."

"Nothing is as important as the spear." The moment I said the words, I regretted them. Even if what I said was true, I could see the hint of disapproval in Asher's eyes. He liked it better when I was scared of using the spear. Maybe he thought I could be controlled if I was afraid. But that wasn't going to happen.

"Cassie . . ." Simone touched the side of my arm.

"What?" I snapped, yanking back my arm.

"Whoa, relax." Simone held up both her hands. "I know we're all under stress, but I was only going to point out that the weather can change pretty fast out here and the shore can disappear in a storm, you know? If we can't see the shore, we can get turned around."

"Haven't you heard of a compass?" Asher retorted. "Just give me a few minutes, and let me see if I can make sense of this. We'll go as soon as I'm done."

I was eager to get going, but Simone's words had triggered something that was floating on the fringes of my brain. Like my subconscious was working on an idea that hadn't been shared with the rest of my mind.

The clouds could make the shore disappear, but the shore would still be there. It would just be hidden behind them. Like how some of the letters blended into the background, hidden when I placed the paperweight on top of them.

Aisa, the old woman in the church, had said to see what is unseen.

The letters still existed even though they appeared to vanish . . . like the shoreline.

I looked down at the journal. The clue wasn't in the letters we could still see, but in the ones that had disappeared! Despite my hesitancy to release destiny, a piece of me did want to know what was written in the coded message. It might even help me somehow when I use the spear.

"Asher, it's the opposite of what we're doing," I said. "The message is in the letters we don't see." I looked at Simone. "Do you have more paper in there?"

"What do you think?" Simone smiled and handed me three more receipts. "You know I like to shop."

"All right, let's try this again," I said, ignoring the waves that now pushed against the boat. "Here." I handed Simone the paperweight. "Hold on to this while I look for the letters we didn't use." I balanced the notebook on my lap and got ready to write on the back of the new receipt. "Okay, Asher. Call out the letters I already gave you, and this time I'll write down the ones we didn't see."

Within seconds, the first word was revealed.

A-C-T-I-O-N.

We were on the right track! It didn't take long to write down all the letters and have the complete message.

> *Action has been taken to return destiny to how it was intended*
> *Unconstrained and multifaceted*
> *The world is ablaze with possibilities*
> *No more will it be chained to the choices of one*
> *Second cipher key given to Michelangelo*
> *Master of light and dark*
> *Before going to Rome he placed it with his latest maiden*
> *It is outstretched and present*
> *Reaching out from the darkness*
> *For all to behold and none to understand*
> *Except for you*
> *You will see what is written*
> *And return fire to the world*

"Holy cow." Simone's voice was a whisper of amazement. "We did it. We actually broke the code."

"But it still doesn't mean anything." I pointed to the second half of the solved code. "It doesn't tell us how to do anything." I was upset with myself for even thinking this was going to help. "It just points to another clue or key to a clue. We don't have any real answers. This is a waste of time."

"Yeah, but we're one step closer," Asher replied. "If we can figure this out, too, it could change everything."

"That's a big if," I answered.

"And since when did you become so negative?" Simone asked. "I thought you wanted to do this."

"Sure . . . maybe. But what we really need is to get the spear and start trying to have me change the future."

I noticed Asher and Simone exchange a weird look.

"Listen." I tried to explain myself to them. "I'm not saying we can't do both things . . . only that we can't waste too much time on something that we may not be able to figure out. And even if we could release destiny, who knows if that's a good idea. Wouldn't it be better to be able to pick a future ourselves? A good path?"

"I don't know. Who's to say we know what's best?" Asher pointed out. "We've already made mistakes."

"But that was because I didn't think things through and didn't really know what I was doing. It would be different if I got some training."

"Maybe, but giving everyone a choice and not having the future be controlled sounds much better, don't you think?" Simone didn't wait for me to answer and instead pointed to what I had written. "And we can do that because, apparently, this Michelangelo guy gave the clue to his girlfriend. See the part about placing it with his latest maiden?"

"But giving the key to a woman for safekeeping wouldn't make sense," Asher said.

"Excuse me?" Simone crossed her arms.

Asher rolled his eyes at her. "I don't mean that a woman couldn't keep it safe; of course she could. I mean giving it to one person doesn't make sense. This Guardian is leaving a clue to all future Guardians. So that people in the future— like us—could free destiny if we needed to. That's why it says the cipher, the key to solving the clue, is somewhere for all to behold." Asher stared at the words written on the receipt. "He would have placed it somewhere permanent . . . like on a building or a statue. Not just given it to a girl-friend. It has to be something accessible to future Hastati."

"Hmm." Simone tapped her temples like I'd seen her do in school countless times when she was deep in thought. Suddenly, she jumped, causing the boat to rock back and forth. "I got it! It mentions Michelangelo and going to Rome, so maybe it's about hiding it in the Sistine Chapel or some-where in the Vatican. The spear is connected to Saint Longinus, and there's a huge statue of that soldier inside St. Peter's Basilica. I've seen it!"

"Um, no." Asher shook his head. "That's not it."

"Why?" Simone's expression changed from pride to indig-nation. "Because I came up with the idea and not you?"

"No, because the Michelangelo you're thinking about was already dead and buried by 1610 when this was written."

"Oh." Simone pursed her lips. "Yeah, well then, I guess it's not him."

But the idea of it being an artist resonated with me.

"It's Caravaggio!" I blurted, thankful for all the times my father had discussed the famous painter with me.

Asher smiled. "I was thinking the same thing." He glanced at Simone. "Michelangelo Merisi was Caravaggio's real name," he explained. "He was considered a master in the use of light and dark, like the clue says."

"So Caravaggio was working with the Hastati or one of the Guardians?" Simone asked.

"I don't know . . . maybe," Asher replied. "He got into trouble a lot, and I know he found refuge with the Knights of Malta for a while until something happened that made him flee to Naples."

"And that was right before he left for Rome," I added.

"Okay, art nerds, so where did he put the cipher key?" Simone rubbed her arms as the wind shifted and became cooler.

"I'm not sure, but I'd guess it's in his artwork."

"Do you think he secretly wrote something into one of his paintings, like what da Vinci did with the eyes of the *Mona Lisa*?" I asked, an unexpected excitement bubbling up inside me. As much as I wanted to go get the spear, the idea of solving a centuries-old puzzle was intriguing. Add to that the fact that I might be able to undo everything with one big move and still keep the spear to change future events in case of an emergency or something . . . now suddenly, I had butterflies dancing in my stomach.

Asher's mouth twitched as he considered the idea. "Maybe."

"Um, even at the risk of sounding ignorant again"— Simone glared at Asher, as if warning him not to make a remark—"what do you mean? Because I know the *Mona*

*Lisa*'s eyes seem to follow you as you move around the room, but is there something else?"

"A secret code." I held my hair to keep it from whipping around in the wind. "I remember that my dad was super excited when news of it came out. Art historians found these microscopic letters and numbers hidden in the irises of the *Mona Lisa*. One eye had the letters *LV*, probably representing Leonardo da Vinci's initials, and the other eye had a couple of numbers and letters, but they weren't very clear. No one knows what those mean."

"So you think the key to unraveling the secret message is written microscopically?" Simone twisted a blonde lock of hair around her finger and gave it a tug. "How the heck are we going to see it? It's not like we carry around microscopes."

Asher pointed to the journal. "I don't think this one is microscopic. It says everyone can see it; they just don't understand the meaning. Like it's hiding in plain sight."

"The code says he placed it with his latest maiden before going to Rome." I thought back to all the discussions my father and I had about art. This would have been a perfect time to be able to pick his brain. He could probably figure this out in two seconds.

"Caravaggio never made it to Rome," Asher said. "I forget all the details, but he died before getting there. It was all pretty suspicious."

"So then it's got to be one of his last paintings," Simone mused. "Something in 1610 that—"

Asher smacked his hands together, surprising Simone. *"The Martyrdom of Saint Ursula!"* he shouted. "It's his last work of art before he died. It has a woman being shot in the chest with an arrow. That's his latest maiden. I don't know why I didn't think of it immediately. The cipher key has to be in that painting somewhere."

"So how do we find it?" Simone asked. "It might not be in a museum. Some paintings are held by private owners. I know my mother has a couple of Picasso and van Gogh paintings."

"Wait, I know this one. And I think I've seen it recently." I thought back to the train station in Naples. "When we were waiting for Simone to buy the caps and sunglasses in Naples, I saw a flyer for a museum with a Caravaggio on the front. It was of a woman being shot with an arrow." I squinted, trying to recall the name of the museum. "I think the museum had the name of something weird like the Palace of Shoes."

"I've never heard of that place, and I would know about a palace for shoes." Simone gave me a wink.

"Are you sure about the name?" Asher asked.

"No. I thought it was something like Palazzo Zapatos, but it might be a name that looks like that. If we go back there, we can pick up a flyer and figure it out."

"So are we going back to Naples?" Simone asked.

The cool wind flapped the receipt in my hand.

The sky had grown dark to the north in the direction of Naples, and in the distance, sinister clouds were dragging themselves across the restless sea, edging ever closer to our boat. A bolt of lightning arced from one cloud to another, casting the heavens in a brief but powerful white glow. This was the moment I had seen in my echo tracing.

"No. We need to stick with our plan," I said, stuffing the receipts between the pages of the Guardian's Journal and putting it back into Asher's backpack. "Get the spear first."

"Cassie's right," Asher said while pulling up the anchor. "Going back to Naples would make us head into the storm. Better to stick close to shore and head south toward Positano. If the storm gets too close we can always seek shelter along the coast. We can come back to Naples after we get the spear."

"Exactly." I felt relief that Asher was agreeing with me. Maybe he was having his own doubts about the whole releasing destiny idea. He could be thinking that mankind might choose the wrong path and that it would be better if someone could guarantee a good outcome. Someone like me.

Asher revved up the engine. "Plus, that painting hasn't gone anywhere in hundreds of years, but Simone's mother might move the spear tonight and we'll lose it for good. We have to get the spear first and then look into releasing destiny."

I nodded, but my thoughts were already on how I was going to use the spear to fix the future.

## EIGHTEEN

The threat of bad weather forced us to move quickly, but the storm stayed behind us, which I took as a good omen. Maybe it meant we'd have a little divine intervention in our quest. Pulling into Positano, I couldn't help marveling at how beautiful the town looked from the water's edge. Pastel buildings rose from the shoreline all the way to the top of the mountain, and each one appeared to be resting on the roof of the one beneath it. The domed roof of a church with the cross on top stood in the middle of it all.

We had decided to stop in Positano to make the call to Simone's house since it was the closest marina and would likely have a pay phone we could use. We moored the boat at the end of a pier and crossed the black-pebbled beach to reach the stores and restaurants that lined the strip. Asher and I kept our heads down, even though we were wearing our sunglasses and caps, still somewhat nervous that someone might recognize us.

As we passed the first couple of cafés, a few people walked by us eating slices of pizza. "Are either of you hungry?" Simone asked. "Because I could really go for something."

I was about to say that we should simply find a phone and get back to the boat when my nose caught a whiff of onions and garlic being cooked nearby. My stomach immediately rumbled. "I guess we could get something quick over there." I pointed to a small pizza shop squeezed in between a luggage store and souvenir shop.

"You two get the pizza while I find us a pay phone or a place that sells prepaid cell phones." Asher gazed up the street. "I can be back here in about fifteen minutes."

"Since when do you give the orders?" I said, not liking the idea of splitting up. "Last time we almost didn't find you."

"It'll be faster this way," Asher insisted. "Plus, they're looking for the two of us together. It might be better if only one of us is wandering around." He pointed to an area next to the marina where there were a few park benches. "I'll meet you over there, okay?"

"He's got a point, Cassie." Simone opened her wallet and handed Asher some money.

I did like the idea of saving time. The faster I got the spear, the faster I could start changing things. "Fine. But hurry."

Asher gave me a wink and then fell in with a pack of elderly tourists walking up the narrow streets.

"Now for some good food," Simone declared, taking me by the arm and leading me into the pizza shop.

My mouth watered as we ordered and got our pizza, buying an extra slice for Asher. Balancing the slices on paper plates, we found an empty bench under a tree that was tucked away, out of sight. Within a minute, I had devoured the large slice . . . enjoying every bite of the crispy crust, the rich tomato sauce, and the perfectly melted cheese. It might have been the best pizza I'd ever eaten.

Or maybe I was just famished.

Either way, it was hitting the spot.

"Really good, huh?" Simone picked at a string of cheese that clung to her lips. "Asher better hurry, or he's going to eat his cold. I think he—"

But her words disappeared as a blinding light forced me to close my eyes, and a searing pain shot through me.

It was happening again.

Another echo tracing.

Slowly, the image came into focus. Bodies littering the streets. Once again, I could only witness the events from one angle, stuck with the single camera lens that let me see what had already been revealed, but wouldn't let me turn around to gather more information. I saw the soldiers in hazmat suits drive by the bodies, but this time I noticed an abandoned newsstand on the corner. I strained to get a better look. Then, like someone holding a magnifying glass to a picture, the image of the newsstand drew closer. I could read one of the newspaper headlines—"Mysterious World Epidemic Kills Millions"—but I couldn't make out anything else. A feeling of nausea overwhelmed me. I was responsible for this. My decision to save my dad had caused a ripple effect that would lead to millions dying. This was even worse than I had imagined.

I felt Simone's hands tickling my ribs, and my eyes fluttered open. The echo tracing was over.

"And you're back," Simone uttered, trying to make light of the situation. "You gotta stop doing that. It freaks me out."

"It's not like I have much choice," I mumbled, still feeling a bit disoriented. A cold sweat broke out around my neck. Lunch and an echo tracing made for a bad combination.

"I think I'm going to be sick," I said, leaning forward, my hands on my knees.

Simone pulled my hair back, thinking I was going to throw up. "Just breathe," she said, smoothing the strands from my face. "In and out."

I nodded and did as she suggested.

Simone rubbed my back until the feeling subsided.

"Thanks," I said, sitting up again.

"You're looking a little less green," Simone observed. "But is being linked to the spear making you sick? Is that what's happening to you?"

"The spear isn't making me sick. It's what I've done that makes me want to throw up."

"I don't understand." Simone's blonde, almost-invisible eyebrows scrunched together. "What did you do other than touch the spear?"

Asher wouldn't want me to say anything, but he didn't know Simone like I did. Regardless of how she had betrayed me with her mother, in my heart I knew she'd only tried to do what was right. She was like a sister to me, and I wanted to trust her again.

"I accidentally changed the future," I said. "I just wanted to save my dad, but the path I chose put the world in danger, and now millions will die if I can't change it back."

Simone flinched. "Millions?"

"That's why I need to find the spear and make it right again!" I could hear the panic rising in my voice. "I need to choose a different path."

"Shhh." Simone rubbed my back again. "Okay, okay, that's bad. But it's going to be okay—you said yourself, once you get the spear, you'll just pick a different outcome."

"I know, but the spear only lets me control the immediate future. I have to figure out what choice will create consequences that change the distant future. Create the destiny I want."

"But what happens to you when you get all stiff and can't hear us? Are you trying to make those choices?"

"No, they're flashbacks about the future that I saw. It—"

"You're telling her!" Asher exclaimed.

Simone and I spun toward the sound. We hadn't heard him come up from behind.

"You know she's not to be trusted!" Asher lowered his voice but kept the same intensity.

"How did you . . . ?" Simone's eyes darted around as if looking for an explanation other than the fact that Asher was really good at sneaking up on people.

My eyes went to the bag he was holding. "You got the phone?" I asked, hoping to change the subject.

"Forget that." He pulled me up by the hand and led me away from the bench. "Why would you be talking to her? It's bad enough she's with us."

"You don't understand. I know Simone. She made a mistake and wants to make up for it. Just like me." I put my hand on his arm. "You have to trust me on this. I know what I'm doing."

"I don't think you do," Asher replied, pushing my hand away.

"Well, I'm the one who can control destiny, and I say this is the way things are going to go. Like it or not."

"Hey, guys," Simone tried to interject from her place on the bench.

We both ignored her.

Asher's eyes narrowed. "We're a team. Don't forget that, Cassie. This isn't your show."

"It is my show," I said. "Because I'm the one who messed things up, and I'm the only one who can make it right again. I'm the one who's going to make choices for the entire world."

"But I'm equally involved. I'm bound to you. Something happens to you, and it affects me, remember? You're letting this whole idea of controlling the future go to your head. You're being selfish and stubborn."

"Me?" I couldn't believe he was talking to me like this. "You're the one who refuses to accept that Simone is sorry for making a mistake. Yes, it was a huge, colossal screwup, but she thought it was for the right reason. I trust her. She's like family to me. And at least she trusts me to fix things. You're the one being selfish and bossy. Don't forget that, in the end, I'm the only one who makes the choices, not you!"

Asher and I stared at each other seething, neither one of us backing down from the fight.

"Guys, you may want to see something," Simone called out again.

Asher blew out an exasperated breath and held up his index finger. "Can you give us a minute?"

"Um, no. I need you to look over there." Simone pointed to the sky over the marina. "That's my mother's helicopter headed out. She must've just left the house. Whatever we're planning, it's got to start now . . . if the two of you are done arguing."

I looked out at the sea, where a red helicopter with white lettering on the side flew toward the mountain peak above Positano.

My breath caught in my chest.

I recognized the helicopter. It was the same one that had hovered over us in the woods while the military chopper fired the missile at our cottage.

Simone's mother had been the one to blow it up, not the Hastati! She really was willing to kill me and anyone who was close by.

"Are you sure that's her?" Asher questioned. "And not a Hastati helicopter?"

"I know what our copter looks like," Simone answered. "Why would you think it was Hastati?"

"Because it was in the air when Dame Elisabeth's cottage exploded," I said. "And since the Hastati showed up right after it got destroyed, we thought it was all done by them."

"You see! I told you my mother was trying to kill you!" Simone shook her head. "I can't believe I ever fell for the stuff she told me. She never even paid any attention to me until she found out that I was connected to this whole spear business. And now she's not going to stop until she can control the spear's power."

"That's why I'm . . ." I glanced at Asher. "Um . . . *we* are going to take it from her."

# —NINETEEN—

We decided to call Simone's house with the prepaid cell phone Asher had bought once we were back in the boat. Our plan was to push off from the pier and head down the coast after Simone convinced the guards to go to Salerno. This would give us at least four hours to get in and get out. We were risking everything on this plan. If it failed, Simone's mother would have the spear, Tobias, and me.

Simone stared at the phone in her right hand while biting the nails on her left. I could tell she was as nervous as we were . . . although her mother would probably not try to kill her.

Probably.

"You've got this," I whispered. "Didn't you say your mother only hires English-speaking guards?"

"Yeah, and I can do a pretty good impression of her in Italian, too. It's just that . . . I don't know if . . . I'm not sure if sending them to Salerno is a good idea. What if they ask me for details? I don't know too much about that city."

"But you said your mother sometimes goes to Salerno on business, right?" Asher asked.

Simone nodded, her hand shaking a little. She knew our entire plan hinged on her convincing the guards that she was her mother. "It's just that if they start asking questions, I don't know the streets and stuff. I could pull it off a little better if it were Rome."

"Yeah, but your mother wouldn't demand that these guards leave right away to meet her all the way in Rome," I reminded her. "She'd just get people from over there."

"Salerno makes sense. It's far enough that it'll take them a couple of hours by boat, our paths won't cross because they're heading away from us, and they know your mother goes there." Asher paused. "But if you don't think you can do it . . ."

"She can do it," I insisted, and squeezed Simone's arm. "Just take a deep breath and call."

Simone inhaled and exhaled slowly. "Of course I can do this," she said in her mother's voice. "I'm Sarah Bimington. No one questions me." Then she dialed her house.

Asher and I stared as the seconds ticked away. Simone gave a small nod as soon as someone answered the call.

"Yes, who is this?" Simone's voice had an irritated tone to it, just like the one her mother might use. "Lorenzo, you say? Fine. This is Sarah Bimington. There's been a change of plans. I need you and all the other guards to come to Salerno right away."

Simone listened as the person on the other end spoke. The voice was low and rumbling, but I couldn't make out what was being said.

"Yes, of course I realize that Tobias will be there with only the house staff. Are you questioning my orders?" Simone gave me a wink. She was on a roll. "I thought so. Now, I need everyone to go wait for me outside the Deutsche Bank. Do not call me, as I want no trace of communications. I will contact you when I am ready to proceed, is that clear?"

Simone waited for acknowledgment, but her eyes widened in panic.

"Which branch?" She widened her eyes as if we might be able to tell her which locations existed in Salerno.

Asher shrugged.

I had no idea, but I remembered the answer Simone gave the cabdriver, which was specific but still vague. "Main branch," I suggested.

Simone shook her head. "Which one do you think?" Simone said, flipping the question on the guard. After a short pause, she answered, "Of course, I'm referring to that one. And my daughter will also be returning to the house with some friends." Simone took a breath. "No, I don't want them detained! I don't care what my prior orders were." Her voice almost broke out of character, but she composed herself. "Everyone is to do as my daughter requests. She has my full authority. Now, hurry up and get to Salerno."

She ended the call and let out a big sigh. Her hands were still trembling, but she had a smile on her face.

"You did it!" I exclaimed, giving her a quick hug.

"Not bad," Asher muttered. It was high praise coming from him. He pushed the boat away from the pier. "Now let's see if you're right about the spear actually being there. I'd hate to think this is all for nothing."

"It's there," I said. "It has to be."

It only took us about thirty minutes to get to Simone's house, which, as she had described, resembled a fortress sitting at the top of a massive, three-hundred-foot-high outcropping of stone.

Asher slowed the boat as we approached the small cave where Simone said we could moor.

My heart beat a little faster.

Inside the sea cave, stairs would take us directly up to the house. I knew that this could be the part of my vision where I'd meet Tobias by the window.

I took a deep breath. Trickles of cold sweat ran down my side.

We had to be ready for him. The element of surprise was on our side, but we couldn't let him warn Simone's mother. He was a killer who had been able to shape the future . . . he was capable of anything.

"Remember, everyone thinks your mother sent you to the house, so make sure they listen to whatever you say," Asher told Simone as he slowed down the boat.

Simone arched a single eyebrow. "They always listen to me. We just need to go straight to the master suite because that's where my mother has her safe, so it's probably where she put the spear."

"Probably?" Asher questioned her. "You're not even sure?"

"I'll know if it's there," I said, thinking about how even back in the garden of the Knights of Malta, before I was bound to the spear, I'd felt a certain connection . . . an attraction toward it. "Being that close, I'll be able to sense its pull."

"I hope so," Asher replied, not sounding very convinced. "Okay. Everyone ready?" he asked, maneuvering the boat into the dark sea cave that was only illuminated by a spotlight near the stone stairs.

"Guess so," Simone replied, jumping off the boat onto the small dock and tying the boat's rope around the cleat on the floor.

"*Si arrestino!*" a voice from the shadows shouted in Italian. Footsteps pounded down the stairs toward us. In English, he repeated, "Stop!" As he stepped out into the yellow glow cast by the spotlight, the hulking figure in uniform pointed his gun at all of us. "Don't move, or I'll shoot."

# —TWENTY—

Simone turned to face the gunman. "You'll do what?" she asked in a superior tone.

The guard lowered his gun. "Oh, I'm sorry, Miss Bimington. I didn't realize it was you."

"Apparently," Simone answered with all the coolness of an ice queen. "Now put away that gun. You might hurt someone with it."

"Yes, miss." He eyed Asher and me before placing his weapon back in the holster under his jacket. "Your mother left word you might be coming."

"Good. We want complete privacy." Simone motioned for Asher and me to get out of the boat. "Make sure that we are not disturbed . . . by anyone."

"Yes, miss."

"How many people are here?" Asher asked.

Simone shot him a look. Asher needed to remain quiet.

"Same staff as usual," the guard replied eyeing Asher with suspicion. "Why do you ask?"

Asher fiddled with the boat's rope. "No reason."

"We're going up to the house," Simone declared to the guard. "I want you to stay here and keep an eye on our boat."

"But—"

"But nothing." Simone followed us as we headed to the

stairs. "You don't want me to tell my mother that you didn't follow orders."

"No, Miss Bimington, of course not. I will take care of the boat."

"Good," Simone answered as we all hurried up what seemed like a thousand steps.

Finally, we reached a white door. My calves burned after going up so many flights of stairs, even though we'd stopped three times to catch our breath.

"Okay, now that we got over the first hurdle." Asher pointed to the door in front of us. "What comes next?"

"We go straight to my mother's room. It's on the second floor, and she has her personal safe there. I'm pretty sure that's where the spear will be."

"Do you know the combination?" I asked, realizing that this was probably a question I should have asked earlier.

"I can guess," she replied with a hint of disgust. "It's the most important date in my mother's life."

"March fifteenth?" I offered. Simone's birthday.

"Not even close." She opened the door, and we stepped into a large foyer with a black-and-white-checkered floor and the largest chandelier I'd ever seen. "It's November fourteenth. The day she made her first billion."

"Oh," was all I managed to say. I couldn't imagine having a parent like that. I knew with all my heart that I was the most important thing in my father's life. Not just because he told me, but because he showed me. But then again, I'd just discovered that I had a parent who was a murdering madman who would likely kill me in order to regain the spear's power. Perhaps not choosing Simone's birthday wasn't that big of a deal.

"It's up there." Simone drew our attention to a dark wooden door at the top of a wide white marble staircase.

"Then let's go." Asher sprang up the stairs, taking them three at a time. I didn't know where he got the energy.

Arriving at the top, he waited in the hallway until we got there before trying the doorknob. It was locked.

"It's in there." I clenched and unclenched my fists. A sensation that I could only describe as a magnetic pull urged me to go into the room. "I can feel it. The spear is definitely there."

"I can kick the door in." Asher took a couple of steps back, but as he lifted his leg, Simone blocked his path.

"Are you stupid or just a brute?" She shook her head and rapped lightly on the door. "If it's locked, it probably means someone is inside. My mother keeps things on a pretty tight leash around here. She might have another guard or—"

The door swung open, but it wasn't a burly guard who opened it. It was a petite woman dressed in a white nurse's uniform.

"Can I help you?" she asked.

"I'm Simone Bimington . . . Sarah Bimington's daughter."

"Mm-hm." The nurse didn't seem to care much about who Simone was.

"We need to go into the room," Simone explained. "My mother called ahead."

The nurse stepped aside, but her body language told me she was suspicious. It was in the tilt of her head, the crossing of her arms, and the pursing of her lips. She wasn't going to be as easy as the guard who was still in the sea cave. "I did not speak to your mother."

"Well, that doesn't matter. You can go," Simone said dismissively. "You'll be paid for the day."

"I'm not leaving my patient," the nurse retorted.

Her patient. It was probably Tobias. My biological father was only a few feet away.

I glanced around the nurse, trying to see past the slightly opened double doors of the sitting room and into the bedroom. Curiosity pushed me to catch a glimpse of the man I was related to. A monster who killed people and had driven my mother into hiding.

Suddenly, an anger that I didn't recognize swelled inside me. My mother had deserved better.

"You have to go." Simone sounded like she was pleading with the nurse, not commanding.

"Well, I'm not," the nurse replied. "Even though his recuperation is nothing short of a miracle, he's still not strong enough to be left completely unattended."

Asher grabbed the nurse by the arm and twisted it behind her back. "I'm sorry about this." He pushed her toward the bedroom.

"What are you doing?" The nurse tried to get away, but Asher had a tight hold on her.

I followed them into the bedroom and saw the figure from

my vision standing by the window leaning against a chair. He was looking out at the sea and didn't even notice us at first.

Simone rushed to close the bedroom door after closing the one to the sitting room. She pressed a button, and a second metal door slid across the doorway, sealing the room.

"Let me go!" the nurse yelled. Finally, the man by the window turned to face us.

It was here.

Time had caught up to what I'd seen in my vision.

But now that the moment had arrived, I didn't know what to do.

Part of me wanted to attack him, while another part wanted to run away.

I did nothing, simply letting my eyes lock with his.

Tobias had dark hair and a worn, haggard look to his face. He was very thin and didn't seem very threatening. He was definitely not the intimidating monster I had imagined.

"Make any noise and you'll regret it," Asher threatened the nurse. He shoved her into a closet, closed the door, and slid a chair under the doorknob to trap her inside.

"Amanda?" Tobias stumbled against the bed as he called out my mother's name.

My heart hurt at the mention of her name . . . especially coming from him.

"No, it can't be." He shook his head and sat down. "But you look so much like her."

"The safe is over here." Simone went over to where a

Picasso hung next to a gold-framed mirror. "Help me get this painting off the wall."

"Wait a minute." Asher dropped his backpack and pulled out the duct tape. "Hold out your hands," he told Tobias. The man seemed to be in no condition to fight. In fact, he could barely stand.

Tobias sat on the bed and did as Asher instructed, but he continued to stare at me. "You know who I'm talking about, don't you? You have to be related to Amanda."

I ignored his question and went to help Simone. The painting was heavier than I'd imagined. It would take both of us working together to lift it off the hooks.

"Please . . . tell me if she's here," Tobias begged. "I need to see her. Explain things to her. It's been too long."

Everything felt wrong. I'd expected someone crazed with anger or obsessed with power, someone who'd tried to destroy the world. Not this weak and broken man.

I glanced back at him as Asher cut off a piece of duct tape and began to tie his ankles together. It seemed like I should say something, but what?

Before I could think of anything, a searing pain blinded me. I fell against the wall, my hands dropping to my sides as I let go of the painting.

*Not again*, I thought. I frantically fought to stay in the present, but it was no use. I slipped into the vision. In it, I saw something that had flashed by too quickly for me to really notice before: Simone's mother, sitting in an underground bunker, surrounded by TV screens blaring reports about mass casualties all over the world.

*Blegh!*

I sputtered and spat out water.

My eyes popped open, and I found myself sitting on the floor, my face dripping. Asher stood in front of me, a bunch of flowers in one hand and an empty vase in the other.

"A little help over here," Simone eked out while trying to balance the painting against the wall.

Asher tossed the vase and flowers on the bed and rushed to help her with the Picasso. I knew I should help them, but the episode left me feeling dizzy and drained.

"You just had an echo-tracing episode. You're the one who's bound," Tobias declared, his eyes were wide with surprise. "You stole the power from me!"

"Tape his mouth or something," Simone said as she and Asher set the painting down on the floor. "Before he alerts the staff."

But it was too late. Tobias was piecing it all together. "You're Amanda's daughter, aren't you?" He didn't wait for confirmation. "You have to be. And if you're marked, then it must be because I'm . . . I'm . . ." He didn't finish his thought, letting it instead float in the space between the two of us.

I stood, using the wall for support.

"She never told me," he muttered to himself. "Not that I blame her. I was out of control." He shook his head in disbelief. "But a daughter. I have a daughter."

Simone walked over to stand next to me. "Does he really think he's your father?" she whispered. Then, seeing my reaction, she took a step back. "It's true?"

Asher cut a strip of duct tape to cover Tobias's mouth.

"No, don't silence me. I have to explain what happened, so you can tell Amanda. Make her understand." He squirmed on the bed even though his hands and legs were tied. "You also need to know the dangers of using the spear."

Asher drew closer to him, the duct tape stretched out between his hands.

"The choices I was making . . ." Tobias called out. "It was because I was trying to change the final outcome. I was desperate!"

"Don't listen to him, Asher," Simone said, already standing by the safe. "He's working with my mother."

"No, no. I've only been pretending to be in an alliance with Sarah," Tobias claimed. "I needed her to get the power back to me . . . I didn't imagine my daughter would be the one who had it." Asher hovered over him, trying to not miss his mouth as Tobias frantically thrashed his head from side to side. "Please . . . listen. I only wanted the power back so I could release destiny once and for all. Don't let my daughter become what I was!"

Asher stopped an inch above his face. "What did you say?"

Tobias gazed up at him. "Releasing destiny. There's a way to do it."

"Tell us what you know," Asher said.

Tobias's expression changed. "You've already heard of this?"

I nodded.

"Then you know it's the only way to undo all the events that someone using the spear may have set in motion," he said. "It brings back all the options for the future. I just couldn't figure out who I needed to find in order to do it."

"What do you mean?" Asher asked. "You had to find someone?"

Tobias studied me. "I should be telling your mother these things . . . not you. Where is she? I want to talk to her."

"We're the ones who are here," Asher replied, his hands balling up the piece of tape. No longer wanting him to be quiet. "Just tell us what you know."

"I'm done talking," Tobias stated, his eyes narrowing with resolve. "I want to see Amanda. I'll only speak to her."

"You can't," I replied, not wanting to tell him what had happened to my mother. After everything he'd done, forcing her to leave everything and everyone she knew, he didn't deserve to know anything . . . not even that she'd died.

"I can and I will," Tobias said. "Or you won't get anything further from me."

I stared at him. I could almost see the callous monster right beneath the surface of this frail man. He was not going to manipulate us. He had scared my mother, but he wouldn't do that to me.

"Cassie . . ." Asher was prompting me to say the truth. "He may have useful information."

I hesitated.

Tobias's expression softened. "I understand you being

protective, but I only want to talk to her. Please," he begged, "I have to make things right."

I could tell that this was the thing he wanted most in the world—and I was the one who could crush his hopes. Make him feel a little of the pain he had inflicted on others. Suffer like he had made my mother suffer. It was a small victory, but I was going to enjoy plunging the dagger in his heart.

"It's too late," I said coolly. "She's dead."

His face fell, and I saw his spirit crumbling with the news. "When?" he asked, his voice barely a whisper.

"Right after I was born." Tears were welling up in his eyes. Then, to add a little bit of salt to his wound, I added, "For all I know, your choices may have killed her."

"No, no," he muttered. "She needed to know. I wanted to explain . . ." He blinked, and a single tear ran down his cheek. "I can see things so clearly now that I'm free of the spear." He went quiet, lost in his own thoughts.

"But you can still help us," Asher said. "Tell us whatever you know about releasing destiny."

"And using the spear," I added.

Tobias gazed at me, his head still shaking in disbelief. "What's your name?" he asked me.

"Does it matter?" I replied.

"It does to me," he answered.

"Cassie. My name is Cassie. Now tell us about the spear."

"Are you happy, Cassie?" he asked. "Have you been cared for?"

I thought of Papi and how he had always given me everything I'd ever needed and wanted. He'd only kept secrets because he wanted to protect me. Because he loved me more than anything. "Yes, I am."

"Good. Your mother would've wanted that." He glanced over at Simone, who was busy opening the safe.

"It's here!" Simone exclaimed, pulling out a piece of velvet cloth and unwrapping it to reveal the spear. "We got it!"

"Don't let her have it," Tobias warned. "Keep it away from her. The power will corrupt her. Look what happened to me."

I gritted my teeth. Who did this man think he was? He knew nothing about me. "I'm not you," I said. "I'll only use the spear to make things better."

"No, no, that's what I thought at first, too. But you'll lose yourself in trying to fix things," he replied. "I'll tell you what you want, but you mustn't use the spear. Stay away from it at all costs. Releasing destiny is the only way to truly save yourself and free the world. Anything else is hopeless."

Simone walked over to us with the spear. "Then how do we release it?"

"I . . . I . . ." Tobias's shoulders slumped. "I don't know. That's why you must keep it away from Cassie. The only thing I was ever able to discover was that there seems to always be one person, a linchpin, who if sacrificed could create a future full of possibilities. Every time I thought I found the right person . . . a politician, an industrialist, even a member of the Hastati . . . nothing worked. The final vision I saw only got worse, never better." Tobias looked away, his gaze falling somewhere outside the window. "I convinced myself that their sacrifice was for the greater good. No one understood that I was trying to prevent the apocalypse, not start it."

"So you killed all those people?" Simone handed Asher the spear. "You thought *killing* could free destiny?"

BAM! BAM! BAM!

We all jumped as someone pounded on the door.

"Who's there?" Simone shouted.

"Open this door, Miss Bimington," a deep voice called. "I don't know what you are doing, but the nurse called the house. You can't be in there."

I stared at the closet where Asher had locked up the nurse. We hadn't even thought about the fact that she might have a phone on her.

"What do we do?" Simone's eyes darted around the room. "These are reinforced doors, but they won't stop him for long. Where do we go?"

We were trapped, but I could change the immediate future. I had the power to do that.

"Give me the spear," I told Asher. "I can get us out of here."

"It's too dangerous." He put the spear behind his back. "We can find—"

BAM! BAM! BAM!

"Open this door right now! I'm going to have to call your mother."

"We're going to lose everything. I need to use it . . . NOW!"

Asher scowled but reluctantly handed me the spear.

"NO!" Tobias yelled.

It was the last thing I heard.

The moment my fingers touched the spear, an electric current ran through me, and I fell into a world of deafening silence with a brilliant white light surrounding me. I felt myself drifting on what seemed to be a wave. It felt the same as when I had first used the spear in the Knights of Malta garden.

*Stay calm and think*, I told myself. I wanted a way out of this house. To find a future where we were back on the boat. If only the guard at the door went away or maybe if he fainted. Yes, I liked that idea. I didn't have to really hurt him. Making him go unconscious would allow us to escape, and there'd be no permanent harm. *Yes*, I thought, *that is what I want.*

I focused on this thought, and suddenly I could feel an undercurrent flowing in another direction. I pushed myself down that path and saw the burly guard standing outside our door, collapsing to the floor.

Had I just changed the future? Maybe that action was enough to change all future events. Dame Elisabeth had said every change had consequences.

I couldn't resist going further. I continued moving forward on this new wave to see what lay ahead. Like an old movie playing on a screen that was flying by me, I saw Asher, Simone, and me on the boat.

My heart beat faster. *That's exactly what I want to happen*, I thought.

More images bloomed in my mind.

Through a thick fog, I saw a dark pillowcase being pulled over my head. *What did that mean?*

Before I could think any more about that, the image switched to a scientist in a laboratory working with test tubes.

Oxygen filled my lungs in short little breaths, and my heart pounded like it wanted to burst out of my chest. In the distance, I heard a voice. It was Asher, but I ignored him and forged ahead, wanting to see more of the future.

A future I might have already saved.

The next scene was Tobias running through the streets of Paris, where a long line had formed in front of a hospital. Then the final image from my first vision reappeared. This time, there were more dead bodies, and the men in hazmat suits all stood as if frozen, staring up at the sky.

A high-pitched whistling noise surrounded me. I couldn't tell if it was part of the vision or something that was happening to me.

I gasped for air.

There was none.

An explosion rocked me to the core.

I couldn't breathe.

Death was near.

# —TWENTY-ONE—

Air.

It filled my lungs as I felt my soul being yanked back through space and time. The visions were whizzing by me in reverse order as I fell backward into what felt like a bottomless pit. I heard Asher's muffled voice in the distance but couldn't understand what he was saying. I tried to zero in on him.

And then I was back in my body.

"Get her out!" I heard Tobias shout. "She's been there too long!"

I opened my eyes to find myself lying on the floor again with Asher beside me, holding both my hands.

"She's okay," Simone said. She stood behind Asher, a look of relief on her face.

"Cassie." Asher gasped as if he had run a marathon. "You can't do that. I almost couldn't get to you."

I sat up expecting to feel weak and weary just like after an echo tracing, but instead I felt energized and powerful. "I'm fine," I said, bouncing up and slapping imaginary dust off my jeans. "Unseal the door."

"Are you okay?" Simone didn't sound convinced, but she pressed a button, causing the metal door to slide back.

"I said I'm fine." I headed to the door. "But we have to go. We need to get to the boat."

"I meant Asher," Simone answered.

Turning around, I noticed that Asher was leaning against the bed. He had a dazed look in his eyes, and his face was extremely pale.

"Just a little dizzy." He blinked very slowly and touched his temple. "I'll get it together. Give me a couple of seconds."

"You stayed too long in the Realm," Tobias commented. "You haven't been trained."

"Well, even without training, I was able to do this." I grinned and swung open the door, revealing the guard that had met our boat downstairs slumped on the floor.

Asher looked horrified. "Is he . . . ?"

"Dead?" I finished the question while stepping over the man. The energy I'd felt while in the Realm still surged through my veins. It felt like everyone was moving in slow motion while I was overly caffeinated. "No. Just unconscious. But once we get out of here, I'll have to use the spear again because this time I didn't make any real changes."

"That's because it wasn't a big enough act," Tobias explained. "Matters of life and death are what have the biggest influence on the future."

"Yeah, well I'm going to find another way . . . thank you very much." I turned to Simone, not caring to hear anything else Tobias might say. "Ready?"

"Cassie, you're acting strange." Simone had that "concerned mother" face.

"I'm fine," I repeated. "We just really need to get moving while this guy's still out."

"She's right," Asher agreed. "We don't have time to waste. I'm feeling better."

Asher taped up Tobias's mouth, and then the three of us hurried down to the cave. I wasn't worried about anyone trying to stop us because, in the vision, I'd already seen us in the boat.

Once aboard, I tried starting the engine, but it sputtered and died.

"I can do it," Asher said, moving me out of the way so he could navigate the boat. "I may be a bit wobbly, but I'm still the better driver."

We pulled out into the open sea, and with the fresh air, Asher began to get his coloring back.

"Where are we going?" Simone asked, gazing out to the horizon, where the storms clouds had gathered earlier. The skies were now clear and the sun hung low.

"Rome," I said.

"Naples," Asher declared at the same time.

"Um, which one is it?" Simone asked.

"We're going to go to Rome because my grandmother and dad are probably there," I said. "She can teach me to use the spear to fix the future."

"I don't think using it again is a good idea." Asher looked back at me. "We have no right to mess with these things. It'd be better to be free of the spear and release destiny."

"We do have the clue in the journal that points to the Caravaggio painting in Naples," Simone added. "We're probably closer to figuring it all out than anyone else has been."

"Fine," I said, yielding to them. "Naples is on the way to Rome anyway. But just so we're clear, if we get into any trouble . . . we all agree that I will use the spear again, right?"

Asher and Simone glanced at each other in a way that made me feel uneasy.

*Were they planning something behind my back? Had they been talking about me? Didn't they understand that I had a special gift and was willing to use it to help them?*

"Let's just try to avoid getting into any trouble," Asher suggested as he increased the boat's speed.

We all stayed quiet for a few minutes. I let the sea spray splash against me a couple of times as the adrenaline I'd felt earlier faded. My eyes kept going to the backpack that Asher had put on the floor between his legs. I felt such a strong sensation, a yearning to use the spear again.

I shook it off. The spear was to be used in emergencies only. I had to remember that.

"Um, I've been thinking about something Tobias said . . ." Simone bit the side of her nail. "About how he was killing people because only the death of one person would free destiny . . . Do you think he's right?"

"I don't know," Asher answered. "Maybe in his warped mind that was the only way."

"And he doesn't have all the information," I said. "He may not have any real information at all."

"But what if he's right?" Simone persisted. "I was thinking about something Professor Latchke talked about in history class."

"You remember something from a history class?" Asher smirked.

"I'm not the dumb blonde you think I am, Asher," Simone answered. "And what I was thinking about was how Franz Ferdinand's death caused a snowball effect that led to World War I. Just like the Tunisian street vendor who sparked the Arab Spring. One person dying changed the entire world." She bit her bottom lip. "What if we end up having to do what Tobias was talking about? Bring death to one innocent person in order to save the world. What if that's the only way? Would we do it? Should we?"

I didn't say anything. I couldn't. The thought was too extreme.

But the question lingered.

How far would I go to release destiny?

Wouldn't it be better to decide the world's future myself, without hurting anyone?

Tobias warned us that using the spear would make me into a monster like him—but what if there was no escape from that? Either choice might make me be seen as a villain.

Was *that* my true destiny? To be a monster just like my father?

# —TWENTY-TWO—

Shades of pink, orange, and red streaked the clouds above Naples as the sun dipped closer to the water. We had decided to find a marina other than the one where we had rented the boat, just in case someone had spotted us, and the one with a medieval seaside castle seemed like a good choice. It was close but not too close.

After docking, we walked between apartment buildings that had clotheslines strung from window to window, until we wandered into a tiny piazza.

"We need a map or directions," Asher said, heading toward a restaurant. "I can ask in there."

"Neither of you should go in there. Someone might recognize you," Simone warned.

"It's better if I go in and ask." She pointed to an area between the restaurant and a small hotel. "You can wait for me over there."

"We do stand out." I watched as two men smoking cigarettes went into a different bar across the street. "I think everyone here is local."

"Fine. You go ask," Asher said, taking off his backpack and switching it so that it now hung from his chest.

"Palazzo Zapatos is the museum name you remember, right, Cassie?" Simone verified. "Palace of Shoes?"

"It's something like that, but not quite." Two little girls

ran around, chasing pigeons in between the chairs of the outdoor café, while their mother continued to one of the main doors of the apartment building. "The museum is Palazzo Z-something. That's really all I remember."

"Just hurry up," Asher said in a low voice. He pulled his Juventus cap down a little lower as an old man with a cane strolled past. "We're gonna get noticed out here."

I thought about the spear. Would using it help? Maybe I could see the museum's location, find out if it was safe for us to go there. It might be better than asking someone.

My hand tingled, as if it was craving the spear. It was so close to me now.

"Let's stand over by that wall," Asher suggested as Simone darted to the restaurant. "We'll be less obvious." Once there, he stood in front of me, his hand against the wall and his back to the street, concealing me.

"What did you see this time when you used the spear?" he asked, his voice just above a whisper.

"Different things." I had to tilt my head up to look into Asher's greenish-gray eyes. He looked at me intently, not with curiosity but with concern. I couldn't forget that his fate was tied to mine. He deserved to know everything. "I saw the guard passing out. Then I saw us in the boat headed to Naples."

"Uh-huh. So that's already happened. What else?"

"I was somewhere foggy, and someone slipped a black pillowcase over my head. The next things I saw were a scientist in a lab and Tobias running through Paris."

Asher grimaced. "That doesn't sound very good. What about all the people dying in the streets?"

My shoulders slumped, and my head dropped. "That still happened," I muttered. "The only difference was that this time there were more bodies, and the people in the hazmat suits were staring up at the sky and then there was a big explosion."

"Like a bomb?"

"I don't know." I rubbed my temples. "That's when you pulled me out. I should use the spear again to try to see more and change—"

"No." Asher didn't let me finish my sentence. "You are not going to use the spear again until we try to free destiny. We're messing around with things that we don't fully understand."

"But that was the whole point of getting the spear . . . to fix things!"

"But what if you're only making things worse?" Asher got closer to me. "It's not worth the risk when we might have another solution. We can wait until—"

"You two look very cozy over here," Simone teased, sticking her head under Asher's arm. "But we need to figure out something for the night. The museum is closed until tomorrow morning."

Asher took a couple of steps back so that we could all face one another. "Are you sure?" he asked. "Did they know which museum you were talking about?"

"Yep." Simone nodded. "And it's Palazzo Zevallos." She gave me a wink and a smile. "Not Zapatos." Simone pointed inland. "The museum is toward the middle of the city. I was hoping it might be in that seaside castle we saw, but it's not. That place is called Castel dell'Ovo."

"Castle of the Egg?" I asked, unsure if I was translating it correctly.

"That's what they told me."

Asher looked around. "So, we need to find somewhere to spend the night."

"I ordered some pasta for us at the restaurant. It'll be ready in about ten minutes." Simone glanced at the mostly empty tables in the plaza. "We can eat it here or take it with us, but I figured we needed to have dinner at some point."

Asher frowned. "We can't stay here. Your mother probably already knows we took the spear, and she'll be searching for all three of us. Nowhere is really safe."

"Another church?" Simone suggested.

I shook my head. "If nowhere is safe, then we have to go to the middle of nowhere."

"Huh?" Asher and Simone responded in unison.

"The sea," I explained. "We stay on the boat and anchor it somewhere secluded. There are plenty of desolate coves along the coast."

"Good idea." Asher nodded in approval.

It was settled. The sea would be our home for the night.

# —TWENTY-THREE—

I woke before sunrise, while the stars still twinkled and danced in the sky. Lying on the boat, a life jacket for my pillow, my thoughts carried me back to my childhood.

Papi could have told me the truth about who I was so many different times, and yet he had kept it from me. He had been searching for the spear for years, and I had found it in just a few days. Maybe it was because I had always been the one who was supposed to find it. Everyone spoke of destiny. Maybe this was mine. To be the one to choose the future path.

"How long have you been awake?" Asher asked, one eye still closed. He had slept with the backpack under his head.

"A while," I replied, noticing that the sky was beginning to lighten and that dawn would soon break. "We still have a few hours before the museum opens. You should go back to sleep."

He stretched out his arms and sat up. "Everything okay?"

"Yeah." I chuckled. "Sure."

"What's so funny?"

"You," I said with a smile. "Everything's okay if you ignore the fact that we're being chased by assassins, your life is bound to mine, and that most of mankind will probably die soon. Other than those few pesky details, everything is awesome."

"Yeah," he muttered, lying back down and closing his eyes. "Stupid question."

Eventually, after the sun came up, we headed back to port. We docked, and having picked up a tourist map the night before, we ventured out toward the center of town.

We crossed a few main avenues and entered a maze of narrow, cobblestoned streets. Café owners were serving breakfast outside on small tables and several stores had already opened their doors. Everything was still relatively quiet, with only a scattering of people out on the street. It seemed that most of the locals were inside the balconied apartments that surrounded us.

Finally, we hit upon Via Toledo, the street where we'd find the museum. We hurried as nearby merchants pushed back the gates that had protected their business's front doors, and the lights inside store windows flickered on.

"That's it right there." Simone pointed ahead. A set of large arched doors was framed on either side by banners draped from third-floor balconies. One banner advertised a new exhibition of Renaissance art, and the other featured a close-up of Saint Ursula clutching an arrow at her chest with the name *Caravaggio* printed boldly in white at the bottom.

Then I noticed the person standing just inside the doorway, and my heart sank.

It was a security guard. He could be aware that the police were looking for us. He might even be on the lookout.

"The first floor is a bank," Asher muttered. That's when I noticed the ground-level windows held advertising for financial products.

"Are we sure it's here?" I asked. "Maybe there's another entrance."

Just then, a group of tourists led by a woman in a large red hat entered through the main doors. The guard didn't even take notice of them.

"It has to be in there. Come on, and don't make eye contact with the guard." Asher hurried across the street with Simone and I close behind.

All three of us kept our heads down as we entered the building. The tour group huddled in the middle of the enormous three-story courtyard, which was covered by a glass ceiling. All around us were smaller archways that had been converted into banking offices. Off to one side, a large marble staircase led to the second-floor breezeway overlooking the lower level.

*"Permesso."* A janitor motioned for me to get out of the way as he carried a couple of folding chairs toward a small temporary stage at the edge of the courtyard.

"We need tickets for the museum," Simone whispered. "I'll go buy them. Stay here."

Asher handed me a pamphlet from a small table in the corner of the room. "According to the brochure, there's going to be some sort of discussion on lesser-known Baroque artists in a couple of hours," he whispered. "That means there'll be more people here. We need to hurry."

I flipped through the brochure. On the back page, I found a basic layout of the gallery with descriptions of what could be seen in each room. The only one we were interested in had a star by the name *Caravaggio* and was on the floor right above us.

About two minutes later, Simone came over and handed us tickets. "I don't think anyone is checking if we have tickets, but just in case."

"It's right upstairs. Let's go." I raced over to the marble staircase.

We passed several ornate rooms, each one painted a different color, but none held the painting. Finally, we came to a light blue room at the end of the breezeway. From its ceiling hung a large, elaborate chandelier, and delicate stucco along the walls reminded me of fancy icing on a cake. Against the far wall, behind a glass barrier about three feet tall, was a single piece of art: Caravaggio's *The Martyrdom of Saint Ursula*.

Even though the painting was the key feature of the museum, the room itself was empty. The tour group that had come in before us was still busy with other exhibits. We approached the painting, staying behind the barrier in case there was some sort of alarm.

"Are we sure this painting is what the code was talking about?" Simone asked. "Because I don't see anything particularly impressive."

Simone was wrong. The painting itself was impressive. The technique Caravaggio used with shadows and light made it a masterpiece. Saint Ursula was touching the arrow protruding from her chest, her skin a ghostly white because she had just lost her life.

"Look." Asher pointed to the top right corner of the masterpiece. "See the man behind Saint Ursula? That's a self-portrait of Caravaggio. And check out what he's holding."

"Is that a . . . spear?" Simone's voice was full of amazement.

"Yep." Asher nodded. "I bet it's a way of telling us that the cipher is here. The question is where? The end of the riddle said that the cipher key was 'outstretched and present, reaching out from the darkness, for all to behold and none to understand.' So, what do we see that others looking at this painting would take for granted?"

"What you just pointed to . . . the spear." Simone leaned closer. "Most people wouldn't know it's a reference to the Spear of Destiny."

"Maybe." Asher stared at the painting. "But I feel like we're missing something."

"Wait a minute. Look what it says here in the description of the painting." I read from a small plaque attached to the wall. "The painting was restored in 2004, and that's when they discovered the hand in the middle. Someone had painted over it. It had been covered up for centuries." I stared at the outstretched hand that seemed to come straight at me. It didn't seem to belong to anyone in the painting.

"It's like a ghost hand." Simone tilted her head to get a different perspective. "Just popping out from the shadows."

"That's it!" I exclaimed. "The code said it was reaching out from the darkness for all to behold and none to understand!"

"Okay, the code's right: I don't understand. Now what?" Simone stared at me, but I didn't have any more answers.

I turned to Asher, who stared intently at the painting. "Asher? You haven't said anything. Don't you think it's got something to do with the hand?"

"Maybe." He seemed lost in thought. "I don't know. The only thing I can come up with is that the hand has the fingers outstretched, almost like it's showing us the number five. That might mean something."

"Sooo? Didn't you study all sorts of medieval codes? What do you think it means?" Simone asked.

"Maybe it's referencing every fifth word or every fifth letter in the words that we already figured out." Asher peeled his eyes away from the painting and pulled out the journal with the receipts where we had written the letters. "Or it could be a shift cipher."

"What's a shift cipher?" Simone squinted as she continued staring at the painting.

"A way to break a code. It just means all the letters shift over a certain number of spots. Like an *A* would shift over five spots to become the letter *F*."

Asher sat on a bench in the middle of the room, took out a pen, and began playing around with the words that had led us to the painting, then shook his head. "This isn't working."

"The journal . . . it's in two parts," I said, realizing where the clue could be hidden. "What is seen and unseen."

"What are you talking about, Cassie?" Simone asked.

"It's not in the words that we already figured out . . . It's in the remaining letters," I said. "The shift cipher might decipher the ones that were left over after we solved the first code." I sat next to Asher. "See if that works."

From the breezeway, voices could be heard outside the room. *"Pièce de résistance,"* someone said in French. Then the room filled up with the tour group. They all crowded around the Caravaggio, snapping cell-phone pictures and ignoring the three of us sitting on the bench.

Asher glanced at the group, then went back to the code. Letter by letter, he worked his way through the journal entry, slowly writing out a message.

After the first few words revealed the phrase "To release destiny," Asher smiled. "You were right, Cassie. This is it," he whispered. "I can't believe it worked. This is huge. We may be about to free the entire world's future."

"Well, let's think it through first," I said. "Not rush into anything."

Asher stopped writing to look at me. "Don't you think that it's important for people to have the freedom to make their own decisions and live with the consequences? Good or bad?"

"I'm not sure." It was the truth of what I'd been thinking for a while. Maybe with some training, I could help the world be a better place. Then again, maybe no one deserved that responsibility.

Asher shook his head and continued.

The scramble of letters soon became a complete message.

*To release destiny back to the world, the Realm must be permanently filled by having the one who enters die in selfless sacrifice while inside the Realm.*

I read the message again, as if the words would change with a second reading.

They didn't.

Tobias had been right. A death was required to release destiny.

Mine.

# —TWENTY-FOUR—

This wasn't what I expected. I wasn't even sure if releasing destiny was a good idea, and now I was supposed to die for it?

"Does that mean . . . ?" Simone looked at me, then Asher. Asher nodded.

"NO!" she shouted, causing a few of the museum visitors to turn their heads. "It can't be," she said in a much lower voice. "Cassie cannot die."

Asher stared at the paper, not saying anything.

"Maybe we're missing something . . . another piece of the puzzle," I suggested.

"There aren't any more pieces," Asher replied, his tone very solemn. He folded up the paper, put it inside the journal, and stuffed it all in his backpack. "What's written is pretty clear. I guess Tobias was onto something after all."

"I don't want to die," I said, my voice barely a whisper.

Asher gazed at me. "I don't want that, either," he replied. "Don't forget that my life is bound to yours."

I had forgotten. As my Guardian, if I died, so did he.

"Maybe my dad or Dame Elisabeth can help us with this. They may know a different way."

"So we keep heading to Rome?" Simone asked. "What if they're not there?"

I stared at Asher's backpack. I had found my dad once

before by using the spear. I could do it again. "We could find out for sure if . . ."

Asher followed my gaze. "No. You're not going to use it again. You haven't been trained. Look what happened last time. Things could get out of hand, and I wouldn't be able to pull you out."

"It'll only be for a minute." I reached for the backpack, unable to stop myself now that I'd gotten the idea. My hand seemed drawn to the spear like a fish being reeled in. "I'll see where my dad is and get out. I won't change anything. Promise."

"You don't know what you're doing." Asher snatched the bag back. "We'll find him some other way."

"With the Hastati and Simone's mom after us? I don't think so." My blood raced with excitement at the thought of using the spear again. "There may not be much time left. This will speed everything up."

The leader of the tour group stood outside the archway of the room, directing everyone to follow her to the next exhibit.

"We shouldn't mess around with the spear. We don't know enough about it," Asher argued, his voice low as the last of the tourists meandered out of the room, taking a few selfies before leaving. "My uncle didn't complete my training. There are lots of things I don't know how to do."

"I know I can do this," I said.

"Cassie's right. Mr. Arroyo may be the only one we can trust to help figure this all out." Simone stood. "I'll keep a lookout in case anyone comes back this way. But you have to be quick about it."

I wrestled the bag out of Asher's hands. He knew it was the best solution and didn't fight me this time. I unzipped the bag. My fingertips tingled with a flood of energy, and I could feel myself quivering on the inside. The spear seemed to be calling out to me, begging for me to go into the Realm, and I was about to give in to that yearning.

Asher held my arm back, preventing me from reaching into the bag. "Just don't stay in the Realm any longer than you have to. Got it?"

"Uh-huh." I thrust my hand into the bag and wrapped my fingers around the spearhead.

Instantly, I felt the now familiar pull into a vast nothingness. *Concentrate on Papi*, I told myself. *Find Felipe Arroyo.*

It felt like a merry-go-round spinning so fast that I couldn't see anything except blurs of colors. Then it stopped, and I saw my father riding in a car with Dame Elisabeth. They were travelling down a road, but I couldn't tell where they were. I tried to figure it out by looking for something recognizable around them, but nothing came into focus.

*Maybe I can skip ahead a little into the future and see where they're going,* I thought. I wouldn't be changing anything.

I pushed myself forward on the same current of energy.

Another image came. Rome. I could see the Vatican's dome in the distance. I knew that place. It was in the garden at the Knights of Malta compound. That's where they were headed.

"Hurry." I heard Asher's muffled voice in the distance.

I was about to head back toward him when the image before me shifted again. In the far distance, like a movie screen at the end of a long dark tunnel, I saw the men in hazmat suits.

*It'll only take a few extra moments,* I said to myself.

"Cassie, get out," I heard Asher say. "Right now!"

I would have to return later. I pushed myself back, kicking against the strong current that threatened to trap me in place.

I latched onto Asher's voice as if it were a hand reaching into the Realm.

I opened my eyes.

Asher was sitting next to me, his breath coming in and out in short bursts.

"What were you doing?" he asked. "I thought you were going to be quick."

"I was." The amount of energy surging through my body left my hands shaking. "I couldn't tell where he was and had to dip in a little farther to get a glimpse of the future. To see where he was headed."

Simone glanced back from the archway. "So, where is he going?"

"Knights of Malta compound," I answered, taking a deep breath to calm myself. "Just like we thought. But I don't know how to reach him without getting caught."

Asher rubbed his hands together and then shook each one out. "We need to figure out a better way for me to get you out of the Realm. It feels like a million volts of electricity just ran through me."

"Sorry," I muttered, realizing that my delay in getting out had physically hurt him.

"The tour group is leaving," Simone said, sticking her head out into the breezeway. "We might want to go out with them."

"Yeah, sure." I looked at Asher, aware that as invigorated as the spear made me feel, it had the opposite effect on him. "Are you okay to go, or do you need a couple of minutes?"

He shook out his hands. "I'm fine. It wasn't too bad this time."

"They're headed toward the stairs." Simone waved us over. "Come on."

The three of us left the room and blended in with the last of the tourist group.

As we went down the grand marble staircase, I noticed that several paintings had been placed on easels around the stage downstairs. One of them made me stop in my tracks. The face in the painting, I recognized it. It was the woman from the church. The one who had emerged from the shadows and given me the glass flame.

Without thinking, I separated myself from the group and approached the stage to get a closer look. A sign nearby indicated it was all part of a collection of art by Bernardo Mei, circa 1667, on loan from other museums. But how could that be?

I stared at the painting. There she was, all dressed in purple holding a pair of scissors. And the woman to her left . . . I blinked twice. Was that a young version of Signora

Pescatori, the blind woman who had given Asher my mother's jewelry box a few days ago? Was I now seeing things?

"Cassie," Simone whispered, pulling me by my elbow. "What are you doing? We have to go."

"Look," I said, pointing to the woman wrapped in a purple dress.

Simone dropped her hand from my arm. "Isn't that the woman from the church with the skulls?"

A small gold plaque under the painting described it as *Alexander the Great and the Fates.* I glanced up at the third woman in the painting. She looked vaguely familiar. Could she have been the gypsy I'd met back at the subway station when Simone and I were first being chased? The one who had acted so strangely when she saw me and who warned me that choices determine destiny?

"Do you think . . . ?" I wasn't sure if I wanted to say it aloud. "And doesn't the one next to her look like Signora Pescatori?"

Simone shook her head, refusing to go along with my idea. "It can't be. That would make them the Three Fates. They're not real. It's just a myth."

"Kind of like what some people think about the spear," I said.

Before Simone could respond, Asher's hand jerked me away from Simone and the stage. "We have to leave," he whispered, pulling me toward the wall closest to the marble staircase. "The half-eared man is here. The one that works for Simone's mother."

A chill ran down my spine. The last time I'd seen the half-eared man was in the hospital room where he'd tied me up and left us with my unconscious father. He was someone who didn't think twice about hurting or killing someone. How had he found us?

"Are you sure?" Simone asked as Asher ushered the two of us toward the front door, all the while staying close to the wall.

Asher nodded. "He was going up the stairs. I don't think he saw us."

In that instant, the half-eared man darted out of one of the upstairs rooms, and our eyes locked. His expression went from surprise to anger, and he started back toward the stairs.

There was only one thing to do.

"RUN!" I yelled, taking off toward the front door, where the tour group had congregated.

We pushed our way out past the bank guard into a crowd of shoppers wandering along Via Toledo.

"Which way?" Simone called.

I looked right, then left, but I had no idea which way was best. I'd just have to take a chance. "Come on!" I darted to the right, weaving around several people and rounding the corner—only to see two large men in suits waiting for us.

I stopped short, and Simone and Asher crashed into me. One of the large, muscular men grabbed me and the other grabbed Asher.

"Let them go!" Simone screamed, yanking on the man's hulking arm.

"Quiet now, Miss Simone," said a voice from behind me.

I squirmed and turned in time to catch a glimpse of the half-eared man. He was squeezing Simone by the elbow and pulling her away.

"Knock them out," he ordered.

A handkerchief covered my mouth and nose. I fought against the man who was holding on to me. I glanced at Asher. He was kicking and doing everything he could to get out of the clutches of the man who had him.

Everything grew very foggy.

*No, no*, I thought. *This is the fog I saw in my vision.*

I tried to look for Simone, but it was the half-eared man's face that I saw just before a pillowcase was slipped over my head.

# —TWENTY-FIVE—

My legs swung from side to side. My head jostled as I came into contact with the ground. Someone had been carrying me and was now setting me down on a cool floor. I opened my eyes, but saw only darkness. The pillowcase was still covering my head.

"Be careful with her!" said a nearby voice. It sounded like it might be Tobias, but I wasn't sure.

"Yes, sir," another voice responded.

I tried moving my hands, but quickly realized that they were tied together behind my back.

"Sarah will be here shortly." It was Tobias speaking, I was certain now. "Go ahead and take those pillowcases off them."

"Sir, I don't think that's—"

"Take it off, I said. I don't even know why you put it on them. They've already been here and seen me."

The pillowcase was pulled off my head.

I blinked, my eyes adjusting to the light. Asher lay next to me on the floor. The half-eared man yanked off his pillowcase, but his eyes were still closed and his mouth was taped. I lifted my head off the floor and saw that we were back inside Simone's mother's bedroom. The situation felt eerily similar to when the half-eared man had tied us up in my father's hospital room.

"Look who's awake already," the half-eared man sneered. He crouched down in front of me, his cigarette-laced breath smothering me.

I shifted my head away from him and noticed that Simone wasn't in the room. He wouldn't have done something to his boss's daughter . . . would he?

"Where's Simone?" I asked, my voice quivering.

*Don't give in to being afraid*, I told myself. *Be brave and figure something out.*

"Don't worry about your little friend." The half-eared man walked away from me, chuckling to himself. "She's safe in her own room. Her mother will deal with her when she gets here."

Tobias sat on the bed. He had dumped all the contents of Asher's backpack around him and was reading the Guardian's Journal. The spear lay next to him.

"Hey! That's not yours!" I shouted, trying to get up, but only managing to roll around since my ankles were also bound together.

Tobias ignored me and flipped through a few more pages. The receipts where we'd written the clues fell out of the book and onto Tobias's lap.

"Stop!" I called out, but I knew it was pointless.

"Shhh!" The half-eared man scowled. "Be quiet or I'll tape your mouth, too." He then motioned over to Asher. "Plus, you might wake up your boyfriend over there."

Tobias glanced up, and his gaze fell on Asher, who was still not moving.

"How did you find us so fast?" I asked, trying to stall while I came up with a plan.

The half-eared man chuckled. "Ms. Bimington knows many people around here."

Asher began to stir, and then suddenly, his eyes were wide open, and he thrashed around on the ground fighting against the zip-ties that held his hands and feet together.

"Cargh! Carrrghhh!" he called out through the duct tape that covered his mouth.

"Settle down." The half-eared man put his foot on top of Asher's chest to stop him from moving. "Don't make me knock you out again."

"It's okay." I tried to sound reassuring, even though I knew how much trouble we were in. "Asher, I'm over here. I'm fine."

Asher struggled to turn toward me, the half-eared man keeping his foot pressed against his chest.

I despised that man. He seemed to actually enjoy torturing people. My anger overwhelmed all my fears. It kept them buried deep in my gut.

I had the power to control the future . . . Why should I be afraid of anyone? I just needed the spear, and everything would be fine.

"Get your foot off him, Dante," Tobias instructed.

The half-eared man gazed down at Asher and gave him a slight shove with his foot, but reluctantly obeyed.

"Listen," I gazed over at Tobias. "I . . . I don't know what you have planned, but—"

"Ha!" Dante laughed. "She still hasn't figured it out. That's funny."

Tobias didn't laugh.

"The only reason you're still alive is because Ms. Bimington wants to be here to make sure the transition of the spear's power goes as planned," Dante taunted. "I'm sure there will be some unfortunate accident in your future."

"That's enough," Tobias barked. "I want Sarah's daughter. Bring her here."

"Sir, I had strict orders to lock her in her room and keep a guard posted outside her door."

"And now you have strict orders to bring her here."

I glanced at Asher, unsure of what was happening. Asher shrugged as he continued to try to get out of his zip-ties.

"With all due respect, sir, I don't follow your orders. I follow Mrs. Bimington's."

Tobias slammed the journal on the bed. "Then you can tell her how all her plans fell apart because you wouldn't do as I requested." His fists clenched. "This will be on you. You want that?"

"No . . ." I could see Dante hesitating. "But I shouldn't leave you unprotected. Even if it's only these kids. They've been resourceful."

Tobias held out his hand. "That's why you're giving me your gun."

"But . . ."

"Give it to me, and bring me that girl! Immediately."

Dante pulled the gun out from the holster and handed it to Tobias. "I'll be right back," he said, leaving the room.

The moment the half-eared man stepped out, Tobias's shoulders relaxed, and his expression softened. "We don't have much time." He spoke quickly and in a low voice. "I want to help you." He held up the receipts with the clues. "What you've written here . . . about releasing destiny . . . this changes everything."

Silence. We were not going to tell him anything. I wish we'd destroyed those papers.

"If I had only known," he muttered to himself. "I could've ended this long ago. I was the one who had to lose his life . . . not all those people I killed."

My hands hurt. It was like my knuckles wanted to be cracked and the only way to alleviate the discomfort would be to get the spear. I had to get it. It was right there on the bed. I could change things. Alter the future. Change the path we were currently on. This had always been about me, and it would have to end with me.

"Arrghhll!" Asher tried to say something.

"Cassie!" Simone ran into the room and hugged me, helping me to sit up at the same time. "I was so worried," she whispered. "I didn't know what else to do. So I—"

Click. The sound of a gun being cocked silenced her.

Simone and I froze, her arms still around me. Slowly, I peered over her shoulder to look at Tobias. He had the gun aimed at the half-eared man.

The half-eared man took a step forward. "What are you doing?"

"Another step and I'll shoot," Tobias responded, not taking his eyes off him. "You know I will."

The half-eared man stayed still.

"You, Sarah's daughter, go close the bedroom doors," Tobias told Simone. "And activate the security feature like you did when you kept out the guard last time."

I shrunk away from Simone. Had she betrayed us again, except this time she was siding with Tobias?

"Go now," Tobias instructed, raising his voice.

Simone scrambled up and did as she was told . . . closing the doors and securing the room.

"I don't know what you're thinking," the half-eared man said through clenched teeth. "But Ms. Bimington will not stand for a double cross. She will find you—"

"Shut up, and get in the closet," Tobias ordered.

The half-eared man didn't move.

"Dante, you know my history. I have no qualms killing someone to suit my purposes. You have five seconds. One . . . two . . ."

The half-eared man walked into the closet. At the very least, now we only had to deal with one bad guy instead of two.

"And throw out your cell phone before you shut the door," Tobias added.

As the door closed, he pointed to a chair. "Slide that under the doorknob," he told Simone. "And go stand by Cassie."

He waited for a few seconds until Simone crouched down next to me. Then he continued to look through the Guardian's Journal, flipping through the pages at a fast rate.

I was confused. What was he doing?

Simone leaned closer to me. "Your dad, Felipe," she whispered, keeping her eyes on Tobias. "I was trying to tell you earlier. I called him. He's on his way."

"What?" I couldn't believe she'd reached him. "Papi? You spoke to him? But how? When?"

She put a finger to her lips and got right next to my ear. "I had a cell phone hidden under my mattress. It took a while to charge it, but it's what I'd use whenever my nanny tried to punish me by taking away my regular phone." She rolled back her shoulders as if she'd won some sort of battle. "Those nannies were never a match for me."

I stared at her. "But how did you know where to reach him?"

"What are you girls doing?" Tobias asked from the bed.

"Nothing," I replied. "Nothing at all."

Simone lifted her hands as if to prove she wasn't doing anything.

Tobias paused, then went back to the journal.

"You said he was going back to the Knights' compound, so I called him there. Pretty good, huh?"

There was a sinking feeling in the pit of my stomach. "Oh, Simone." I shook my head. "Don't you think the Hastati were listening in? They want me dead just as much as your mom does." Things had just become even more complicated.

"I didn't think we had many options," Simone protested. "And your dad won't let anyone hurt you. He even said that the Hastati had reached some type of accord with the Knights. They're going to work together to do some type of rescue."

"We can't trust them to—"

"You. Sarah's daughter." Tobias pointed to Simone. "Come here."

Simone slowly stood up, her back still against the wall.

"Hurry up. I have an idea." He motioned for her to get closer while keeping the gun pointed at her. "Get this pocket-knife and free Cassie."

Simone looked down at me, then cautiously crossed the large room to get to the bed.

"Quickly," Tobias urged as Simone picked up the knife and ran back toward me to saw off the zip-ties.

"Why are you cutting me loose?" I asked as Simone finished slicing through the zip-ties. "What are you up to?"

"Cassie's your daughter," Simone reminded him. "You can't let anyone hurt her."

"I know," Tobias said. "We don't have much time. Sarah will be here soon, and we have much to do."

"Do what?" I questioned, not trusting any idea this madman might have.

"What I've always wanted. To release destiny," he said.

I rubbed my wrists where the zip-ties had cut into them. "Why would we ever—"

BAM! BAM! BAM!

Someone pounded on the bedroom door.

"Tobias! Tobias!" a woman's voice shouted. "You open this door right now!"

"My mother," Simone whispered, her face filled with dread. I nodded.

Tobias stared at me. "There is only one way this will all work."

BAM! BAM!

"This door better open immediately," Simone's mother warned. "That girl is mine. You don't transfer the power without me."

"NO!" Simone yelled back. "She's not, and we're not opening it!"

"Simone?" I could hear the surprise in her voice. "Simone, what are you doing in there?"

Simone looked at all of us. "Ignore her."

"Listen closely." Tobias spoke with urgency while keeping the gun on us. "We have to do this quickly. We'll only get one chance."

There was more pounding on the door, then silence. Simone's mother definitely didn't seem to be the type to give up easily, so where had she gone?

Tobias sighed, his eyes locking with mine. "I truly wish I could've had more time to get to know you." He touched his Hastati ring, the one just like the ones Asher and I wore. His expression changed. Any hint of kindness seemed to disappear and was replaced with a cold, steely resolve. "Take off your ring, Cassie."

My breath got trapped in my chest. I couldn't move. Did he think killing me was the way to release destiny? Or was he taking the power back for himself?

Asher thrashed from side to side, powerless to do anything.

"She can't." Simone stepped in front of me as if to stop any bullet that Tobias might fire. "It'll kill her."

"Exactly," Tobias replied. "That's why she has to do it. Cassie must die."

# —TWENTY-SIX—

My hands trembled. Tobias was in control and my fate—the world's fate—rested with him. I had to do something to outsmart him, before it was too late. The spear was the key. It was my only chance.

"But didn't you say that all you ever wanted was to release destiny? That's what you wanted to tell my mother, right?" I hoped bringing up my mother would make him drop his guard a little. "If I die without having entered the Realm, it won't work. You have to give me the spear and then I'll take off the ring."

"NNNNNN!" Asher protested.

"Cassie, NO!" Simone turned to face me. "You can't be serious. We don't know if that'll even work. He just wants to get the power back. We can't trust him."

I couldn't tell Simone that I had no intention of sacrificing myself, but that instead I was just going to use the spear to change the future for our benefit.

"No, none of you understand," Tobias said. "I don't want Cassie to die in the Realm in order to release destiny."

"A-ha!" Simone exclaimed. "You see! He *is* after the power!"

My heart fell. I thought I could convince him to give me the spear, but now my only chance was to make a dash for it and hope he had bad aim.

Asher struggled against his zip-ties and his muffled cries could be heard through the duct tape covering his mouth.

"I do want the power, but not for the reason you think." Tobias paused, the gun still pointed at us. "Cassie will die, but then I'll use the spear to save her, just as she saved me, once I regain the power. Then I will be the one to give myself to the Realm. It will be *my* life that is sacrificed." Tobias stared at me as if filling his memory banks with my image. "I'm very glad that fate brought us together. Even for a brief moment. You are strong like your mother. She would've been pleased."

"Wait, you're willing to die to release destiny?" I questioned, not wanting to be sidetracked with talk of my mother.

"It's what I've always wanted. Once I save you, I will remove my ring. I have enough experience that I can still control my body while in the Realm. The sacrifice will be complete, and destiny will be unleashed."

"Mrrrfffgh," Asher kicked at the floor even though his legs were still tied. His eyes were wide and he was violently shaking his head no.

"So, you're willing to kill Cassie on a theory?" Simone asked. "You *are* insane."

"It's not a theory," Tobias answered. "It's written in the codes left by the Guardians. You deciphered them yourself . . . you know what it says."

"But they could have been wrong." I said, sidestepping Simone and inching closer toward Tobias. My body tensed. I was going to have to make a run for the spear.

"Stay put," Tobias commanded, picking up the spear with his left hand and cocking the gun. "The easiest way to change your destiny is to have you recover from the poison, but I'll shoot you if I have to. In fact, I'll shoot him first just to prove I mean business." He took aim at Asher.

I stopped moving, but my eyes remained fixed on the spear.

Tobias sighed. "I've lost everything in my life to this spear, but I refuse to have you lose yourself to the spear's power. I can already see that it has a hold on you. You feel it. I know you do. Even now, with your friend's life at risk, it's calling to you. Telling you that you should be the one to make the decisions. That you have been chosen."

I didn't respond, but what he was saying was true. I had been thinking about how to get the spear even if it meant that he fired off a shot or two. What did this reveal about me? About what I was becoming?

"Sarah's daughter." Tobias turned his attention to Simone. "You are her friend, correct?"

Simone quietly nodded.

"You must make sure Cassie never touches the spear again. This can't all be in vain. She deserves a better life than one that is tied to the spear."

Asher threw his body against the wall to grab my attention. "Rrgghhrrr!" he yelled through the duct tape.

I ignored him. Something made me believe that Tobias was telling the truth. He was the only one who knew what it was like to be bound to the spear and the way he described it was right: I had noticed myself changing over the last couple of days. Was releasing destiny the best thing to do? Could it be done? "If I take off the ring and die, what about Asher?" I asked. "His life is bound to me as my Guardian. Would you be able to save him?"

"Cassie!" Simone squeezed my elbow and drew closer to me. "You aren't seriously considering this? He'd have the power, and you'd be—"

The sound of helicopter blades slicing through the air came in through the open window.

My already fast-beating heart picked up the pace even more.

Was Simone's mom coming in through the window? Or was this another missile attack?

"Listen, I know you don't trust me, but once I have the power and am in the Realm, I'll save both of you, just like you saved me. This will work, but we have to do it now." Tobias pointed the gun at my chest. "One way or another."

"I'll do it! I'll do it!" I shouted, not wanting him to fire the gun. "But the ring won't come off." I tugged on it to show him. "I've tried—before I knew what it did."

The whirring of the helicopter blades filled the room, so loud the windows rattled. It had to be right over our heads.

"We're out of time," Tobias announced. "Push down on the center as hard as you can, then twist it to the right, and you'll be able to pull it off. Do it. NOW!"

I looked at my friends. Asher was panic-stricken, and Simone looked like she was about to cry. There was no way to know if I was doing the right thing or not. Choices determine destiny, but it didn't seem like I had much of a choice. I was either going to die by a bullet or by the poison in the ring.

I took a deep breath and twisted the ring off. As I did, I felt a small prick and a cold sensation ran through my finger. I glanced up at Simone and Asher, the ring dropping to the floor as my hand lost its grip, and I felt my legs go weak. "Cassie!" Simone shouted as my body slumped to the floor. Just as a wave of darkness engulfed me, I saw Asher's eyes roll back into his head.

Then silence.

It felt like I was holding my breath underwater, slowly sinking deeper and deeper to the bottom of the sea.

Everything was so quiet. So peaceful.

I felt like I was being embraced by unseen arms.

Cradled as I drifted toward the ever-growing glow of a golden light.

Then there was a tug, as if someone had lassoed me and was preventing me from going any farther. I looked through the murky waters above me and saw Tobias. He smiled and gave me a nod.

Suddenly, a rush of noise surrounded me as I torpedoed up toward what seemed to be the surface. I broke away from that soothing underwater cavern and took a deep gasp of air.

My eyes bulged open with shock.

Simone was supporting my head in her hands. "She's alive!" she shouted. "Cassie, can you say something? How do you feel?"

"Firghln," I answered, trying to say the word *fine*. My head spun, and I had a hard time concentrating on any one thing.

"Arshrhg," I said, attempting to call out for Asher. I needed to see him. Find out if he had survived, too.

"The poison might still be affecting her system." Asher bent down next to me and took my hand in his. "She's not bouncing back like I did."

A wave of relief washed over me and filled me with new energy. Asher was alive! Tobias had saved us both.

"Well, you didn't get poisoned," Simone pointed out. "You were just a rag doll while I was cutting off those zip-ties."

"You're really okay?" I mumbled, feeling better by the second.

Asher smiled. "Yeah, you can't get rid of me that easy. You think you can stand? We need to get out of here."

I suddenly realized that the helicopter was still rattling the windows. We weren't safe yet.

I sat up, trying to get my bearings, but something else was wrong. There was an emptiness deep inside me that I'd never experienced before.

It was the spear.

My connection to it was gone. I'd lost the power. It felt like I'd lost a part of me, but at the same time, I felt more like my old self than I had in days.

"And Tobias?" I asked. "Did he . . ."

Simone and Asher exchanged glances. "He used the spear to save you, and while in the Realm, he took off his ring."

Simone paused. "He died, but I think he did it. He released destiny."

Tobias being dead meant the part of my vision where I saw him in Paris couldn't come true. Perhaps now none of what I'd seen would happen.

The future was no longer scripted. Free will had returned.

Suddenly, the sealed steel panel covering the bedroom door slid open, revealing only the regular wooden door behind it.

"My mother!" Simone exclaimed. "She got to the main panel and must have hit the override. She'll be here any minute."

Asher helped me stand as I glanced at Tobias on the bed.

I still detested everything he'd done earlier, but maybe I wasn't the daughter of a monster. Maybe I was just the daughter of a man who, in the end, did the right thing. He had released the world and released me.

My eyes drifted over to Tobias. His ring had rolled off the bed and onto the floor, but his left hand was still clutching the spear. My fingertips suddenly tingled and for a moment I thought about picking the spear up. It wasn't the strong urge I'd had while I was bound, but a subtle siren song asking me to use it. An awareness of the power being nearby, up for grabs again.

"Don't even think about it," Asher said, putting the spear in the backpack along with his other things.

Simone opened the doors to the balcony and looked up. I could hear a helicopter whirring up above the building. She waved her arms back and forth.

Asher slung the backpack over his shoulder. "What are you doing?"

"Getting us out of here," Simone answered with a smile. A rope ladder dropped onto the balcony with a thud.

I walked over to where Simone was standing and looked up. Papi was leaning out of the open helicopter door.

# —TWENTY-SEVEN—

I clung to the rope ladder with white knuckles as it swayed back and forth. I had never been a fan of heights, and this was pushing my limits.

"Keep going!" Asher shouted from a few feet below me. "Don't look down!"

Grabbing another rung and pulling myself up, I glanced at my father, who leaned out of the dark blue helicopter, his hand outstretched. It was too noisy to hear what he was saying, but his look of concern was clear.

Adrenaline kept me moving.

As I got closer to the top, I heard Papi's voice. *"Apúrate,* Cassie," he called. "Hurry."

I lifted myself up one more rung and took hold of Papi's hand.

The moment his fingers wrapped around my wrist, it felt like I was finally safe. He pulled me into the helicopter, hugging me tight and showering me with kisses on my cheeks, forehead, and hair.

"I was so worried, *m'ija!*" he yelled, trying to be heard over the chop-chop-chop of the helicopter blades. "So worried!"

Asher climbed inside and motioned to us that Simone was still coming up.

"I got her!" Papi shouted, leaning out the door again.

Dame Elisabeth sat in the copilot's seat next to someone in a gray business suit. She said something to me, but I couldn't hear her. "What?" I shouted.

She touched her headphones and pointed to a pair clipped above my seat. I took the headset off the hook and slipped it over my ears.

"I said that I was happy to see you," Dame Elisabeth said with a smile. "That you are quite tenacious. Definitely my granddaughter."

Papi glanced at her disapprovingly, but then turned to help hoist Simone into the chopper.

Asher put on his own headset and pointed down at the ground below us. "Simone's mother is down there."

I leaned over my dad and saw her standing on the back terrace, screaming up at us at the top of her lungs. Although there was no way we could hear her, it didn't take a lip-reader to realize what she was yelling: "SIMONE!"

As Simone took a seat by the open door facing my father, Papi reached over me to grab the seat belt and buckle me in as if I were a toddler. It didn't matter that we had deciphered a centuries-old mystery, escaped assassins, and had very likely saved the world; to him, I was still his little girl.

And a part of me liked it.

I sat back as Simone put on her headset, and the helicopter banked to the left, heading out over the open water. The three of us looked at one another, Simone and Asher sitting side by side, facing me. It dawned on me that while the power had only been in me, I had never been alone. None of this would have been possible without my friends. We had done it together. Destiny had been released. And now it was all finally over.

Papi squeezed my hand and smoothed back my hair, almost as if confirming that I was really here. *"Estaba bien preocupado,"* he said, his voice coming in clearly through the headset. "I've never been so worried." He shook his head and hugged me again. "When we saw that cottage destroyed, *por poco me muero*." He paused as if his eyes could soak me in . . . making sure that I was really there. "Seriously, Cassie. I almost died. And then when we heard that they had picked up that man at the gas station who was with you, it gave me hope that—"

"Gisak!" Asher interrupted, his voice coming in through the headset. He turned to look at Dame Elisabeth. "Do you know what happened to him? Is he all right?"

"Yes, yes." She nodded. "He's been detained by the police, but we'll make sure he gets released." She tapped the pilot's arm. "Get that done."

It was then that I saw the pilot's profile, and my blood ran cold.

He was one of the men who had shown up at the cottage with the Hastati assassin. We were still in danger!

I tapped Asher's leg and pointed to the pilot. We had to do something, except I had no idea what. We were thousands of feet in the air, and he was at the controls.

Asher scrunched up his face and shrugged. He didn't

understand what I was pointing at. I silently mouthed the words to him: "The pilot was at the cottage. He tried to kill us."

He replied by mouthing, "What?"

I repeated myself, but this time Dame Elisabeth saw as well.

"No need to worry, Cassandra." Dame Elisabeth's voice through the headsets startled me. "Ottavio didn't go to the cabin to kill you, even if our purposes weren't quite aligned at the time. Sarah Bimington may have wanted to kill you, but the Hastati had decided that you were someone who required further investigation. Your fate was yet undetermined, but I've already resolved all that."

The pilot took a moment to turn his head and give us a quick once-over. *"Voglio vedere la lancia,"* he said in Italian. He wanted to see the spear.

"But I saw him there," I argued. "At the cottage."

"Of course, because they were searching for you, but not to kill you," she explained. "We all recognize your importance. And now we've reached an accord where both the Hastati and the Knights will assist in protecting and developing your . . . *abilities.*"

My palms became sweaty. I realized that they still thought I was bound to the spear. That they wanted me to use it.

"You said I would have final say on anything to do with Cassie." Papi's voice had an edge to it.

"Yes, well, plans change. We will gladly keep you posted on Cassandra's progress."

"That's not what we agreed to!" Papi exclaimed. "Cassie is just a girl. She deserves to have a normal life."

"We've already gone over this." Dame Elisabeth spoke through clenched teeth. "There is nothing normal about Cassandra. She is special. I will guide her to her full potential."

"Why, you lying—" Papi leaned closer to the edge of his seat, even though there was nowhere for him to go.

"Please, Felipe." Dame Elisabeth raised a hand to stop him. "Save the melodrama."

*Voglio vedere la lancia,*" the pilot repeated.

"Yes, yes. Give me the spear." Dame Elisabeth held out her hand. "It needs to be authenticated."

None of us moved.

"Cassandra," Dame Elisabeth instructed, "give me the spear. You know that this is your destiny. Don't make Ottavio upset. He can make things more difficult for you . . . and your father. Remember, Felipe is not necessary in our plans."

Perhaps this was why my mother never told Dame Elisabeth where I was. My grandmother was more concerned about the spear's power than she was about me.

My thoughts flew back to the riddle that Dame Elisabeth had given me to solve. The one with the farmer and the chicken. It had all been about thinking things through logically and seeing the consequences of each action. I had to think of this the same way. I knew which outcome I wanted. I might not have the spear, but the future was within my grasp.

"Give it to her," I told Asher. "Dame Elisabeth is right, and I'll need her help to lead the world to a better place." I turned to my father. "I'm sorry, Papi. It's the way things have to be."

"I knew you would understand, Cassandra," Dame Elisabeth said smugly.

Asher hesitated. "Cassie . . . are you sure you know what you're doing?" he asked. I could tell by the way he was looking at me that he had doubts.

"Trust me," I said.

Asher opened his backpack and handed Dame Elisabeth the spear.

She inspected it, then showed the spear to the pilot. *"È la vera lancia."* Dame Elisabeth's voice was laced with awe and hints of amazement.

The pilot took his eyes off the controls for a moment to look at the spear. He nodded in agreement. *"La vera lancia,"* he said. The true spear.

"Pass it to me!" I shouted, gripping the sides of my head.

Dame Elisabeth and the pilot glanced back at me.

Both Simone and Asher had puzzled looks on their faces.

"Cassie." Papi put his hand on my back. "What's happening?"

"Ughhh!" I covered my eyes with clenched fists and pretended to be in agony. I hated scaring my father, but it was the only way. This had to be convincing. "It's an echo tracing." I gritted out the words through clenched teeth. "The spear. Give it to Simone."

I peeked through my fingers and saw Dame Elisabeth exchange glances with the pilot. "It's not needed for an echo tracing . . ." she told him.

My eyes locked with Simone's and I gave her a quick wink. "Ughhh!" I shouted again for added effect. "Please, give it to her. It's critical."

"Hurry up!" Simone reached for the spear, going along with whatever I was doing.

Dame Elisabeth pulled it away from Simone's grasp.

That was when Simone dove into my story, headfirst. "Cassie needs it. In the Guardian's Journal, it says that she could become permanently detached from the power . . . She could die right now!"

Simone was going a little over the top, but it was making Dame Elisabeth reconsider.

"She doesn't have time," Asher added.

Neither of my friends knew what I was up to, but they both trusted me enough to follow my lead.

"For heaven's sake, give it to Simone!" Papi yelled.

"Fine." Dame Elisabeth passed the spear to Simone.

I dropped my hands away from my face.

"THROW IT, SIMONE!" I yelled, pointing to the sparkling blue water, thousands of feet below. "NOW!"

Simone froze for a moment, unsure if she had heard correctly.

I could only hope that she realized what I was planning. With destiny released and no one bound, losing the spear to the waters of the ocean meant that the future would never be controlled by anyone.

Simone flung the spear as far as she could out the open helicopter door.

"NO!" Dame Elisabeth screamed as the spear spiraled toward the sea.

"*Stupida!*" The pilot put the helicopter into what felt like a dive, but it was too little, too late. There would be no way to find the spear in the vastness of the sea. I could already imagine it sinking to the bottom, never to be discovered.

"Why?" Dame Elisabeth demanded. "Why would you do that?"

"She's free," Asher declared, understanding what I'd done. "Now you have no reason to keep her."

Papi looked confused. "What? Cassie is free?"

"I'm not bound to it," I told him. "I don't have the power. We were able to release destiny."

He wrapped his arms around me, not really understanding but happy to wait for further explanation.

But it was more than my being free.

It was about choices. Choices created destiny.

And we'd given the world a choice.

Nothing was predetermined anymore.

Destiny was now in everyone's hands.

# —ACKNOWLEDGMENTS—

Writing this book has been its own kind of adventure, and I'd like to express my deep appreciation to the people who helped bring this story to life.

My first words of thanks go to my wonderful agent, Jen Rofé, who believed in this idea from the very beginning, and to my talented editor, Emily Seife, whose guidance and brainstorming sessions helped me develop the storyline . . . I am so lucky to be able to work with both of you.

Then there are all the incredible people at Scholastic (David Levithan, Lizette Serrano, Saraciea Fennell, Phil Falco, Antonio Gonzalez, Robin Hoffman, Ed Masessa, C. M. Reedy, Emily Heddleson, and Rebekah Wallin—just to name a few) who have welcomed me with open arms. Thank you for your friendship and all the work given on my behalf.

My family, as always, is my foundation. *Gracias* for all your support and encouragement (with special thanks to my son, Daniel, who came up with the title for this book). I am grateful to God for each and every one of you. You give meaning to my life.

I am much indebted to Danielle Joseph, Gaby Triana, Linda Rodriguez Bernfeld, Stephanie Hairston, Alexandra Alessandri, Adrienne Sylver, and Alexandra Flinn, who kept me focused and on track by giving me valuable feedback while I crafted this story. Our critique group is my not-so-secret weapon.

Thank you to Alison Wood Griñan, friend and teacher extraordinaire, for being a sounding board for my plot ideas and for continually reminding me of the impact that a passionate teacher can have on her students. Teachers rock!

Finally, to all my readers who inspire me on a daily basis . . . thank you, thank you, thank you! I get to live my dream of being an author because of YOU!

# —ABOUT THE AUTHOR—

Christina Diaz Gonzalez is the award-winning author of *The Red Umbrella*, which was named an ALA Best Book for Young Adults and called an "exceptional historical novel" by *Kirkus Reviews*, and *A Thunderous Whisper*, which was heralded by the Children's Book Council as a Notable Social Studies Book. She lives in Florida with her husband and two sons. Learn more at www.christinagonzalez.com.